LEGO® NINJAGO

Masters of Spinjitzu

THE CHALLENGE OF SAMUKAI!

PAPERCUTZ™

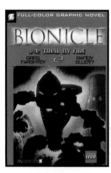

LEGO NINJAGO Masters of Spinjitzu

#1 THE CHALLENGE OF SAMUKAI!

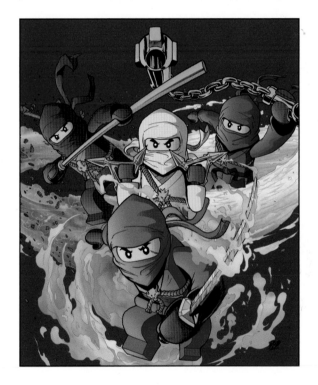

GREG FARSHTEY • Writer

PAULO HENRIQUE • Artist

LAURIE E. SMITH • Colorist

PAPERCUTZ™

New York

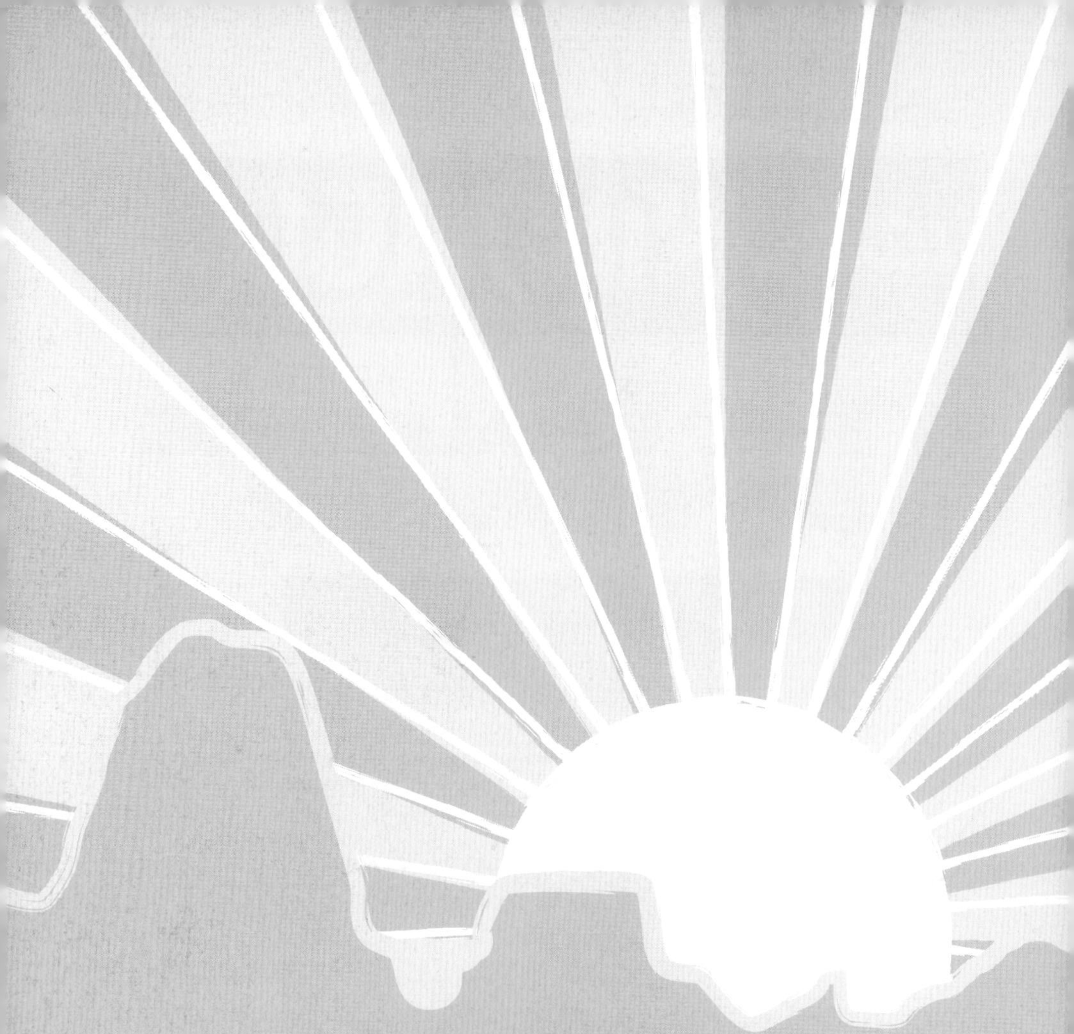

LEGO® NINJAGO Masters of Spinjitsu
#1 "The Challenge of Samukai!"
Production by SHELLY STERNER, Nelson Design Group, LLC
Associate Editor – MICHAEL PETRANEK
JIM SALICRUP
Editor-in-Chief

ISBN: 978-1-59707-297-7 paperback edition
ISBN: 978-1-59707-298-4 hardcover edition

Printed in the US
March 2012 by Lifetouch Printing
5126 Forest Hills Ct.
Loves Park, IL 61111

Distributed by Macmillan
Sixth Printing

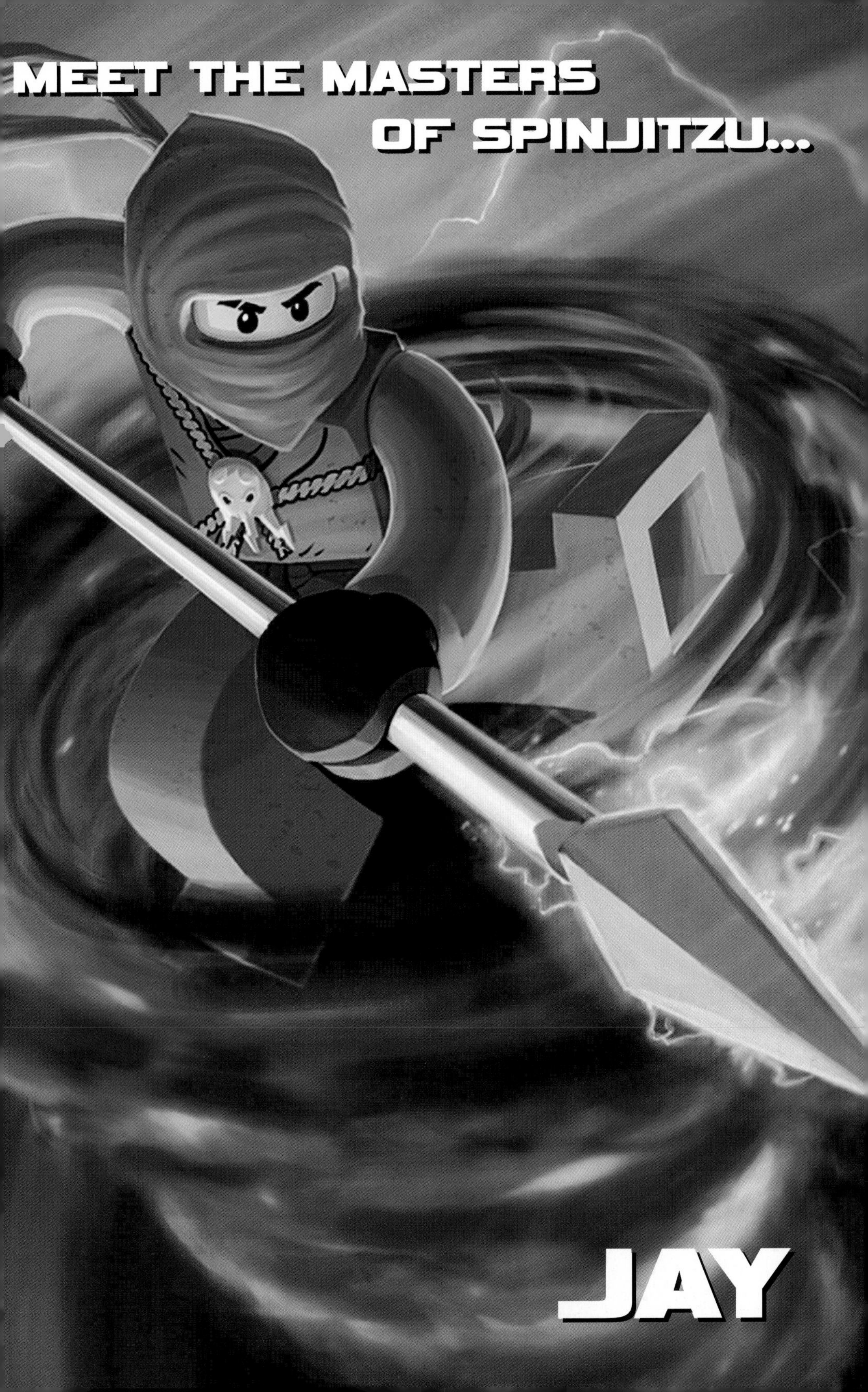
MEET THE MASTERS
OF SPINJITZU...
JAY

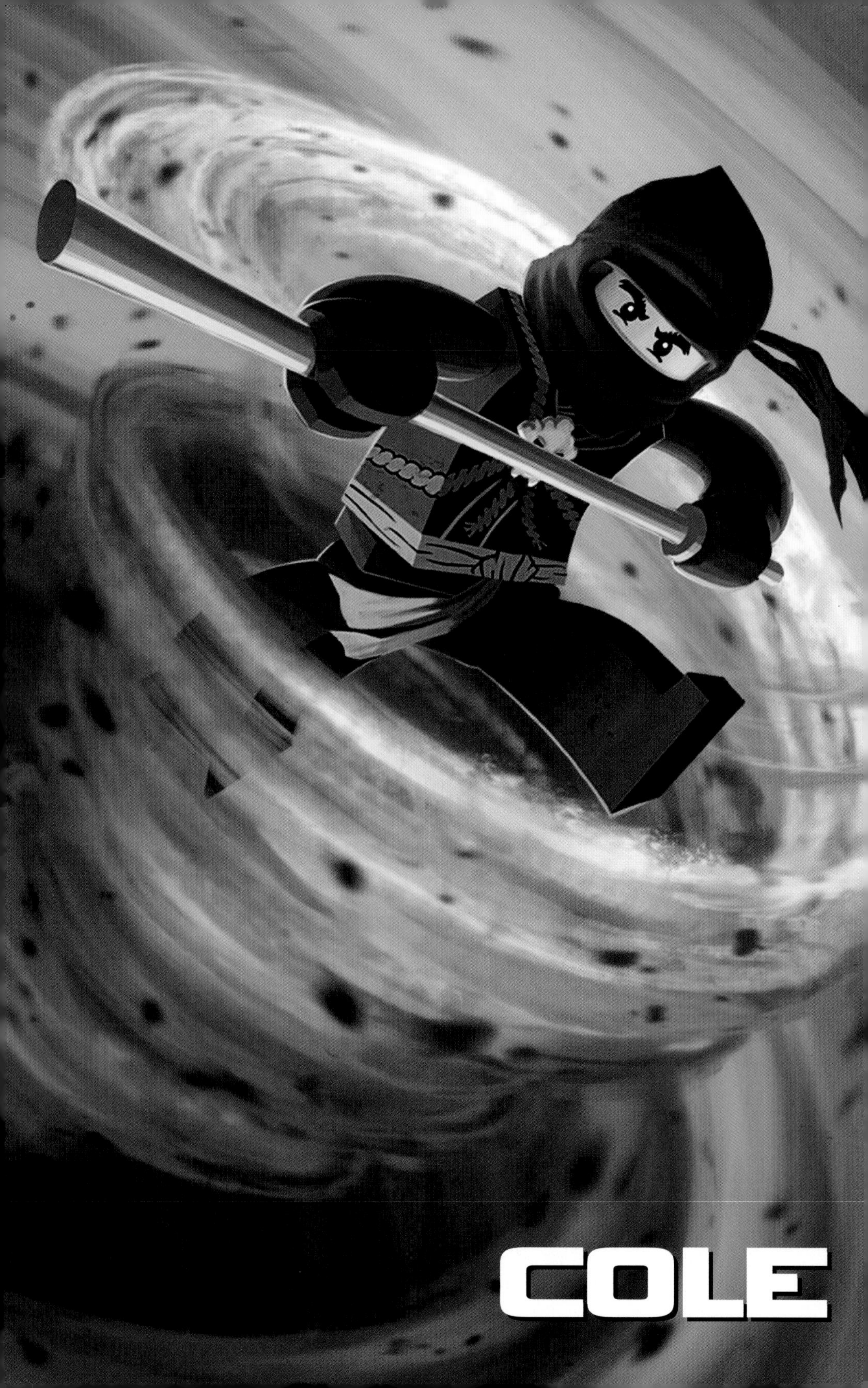
COLE

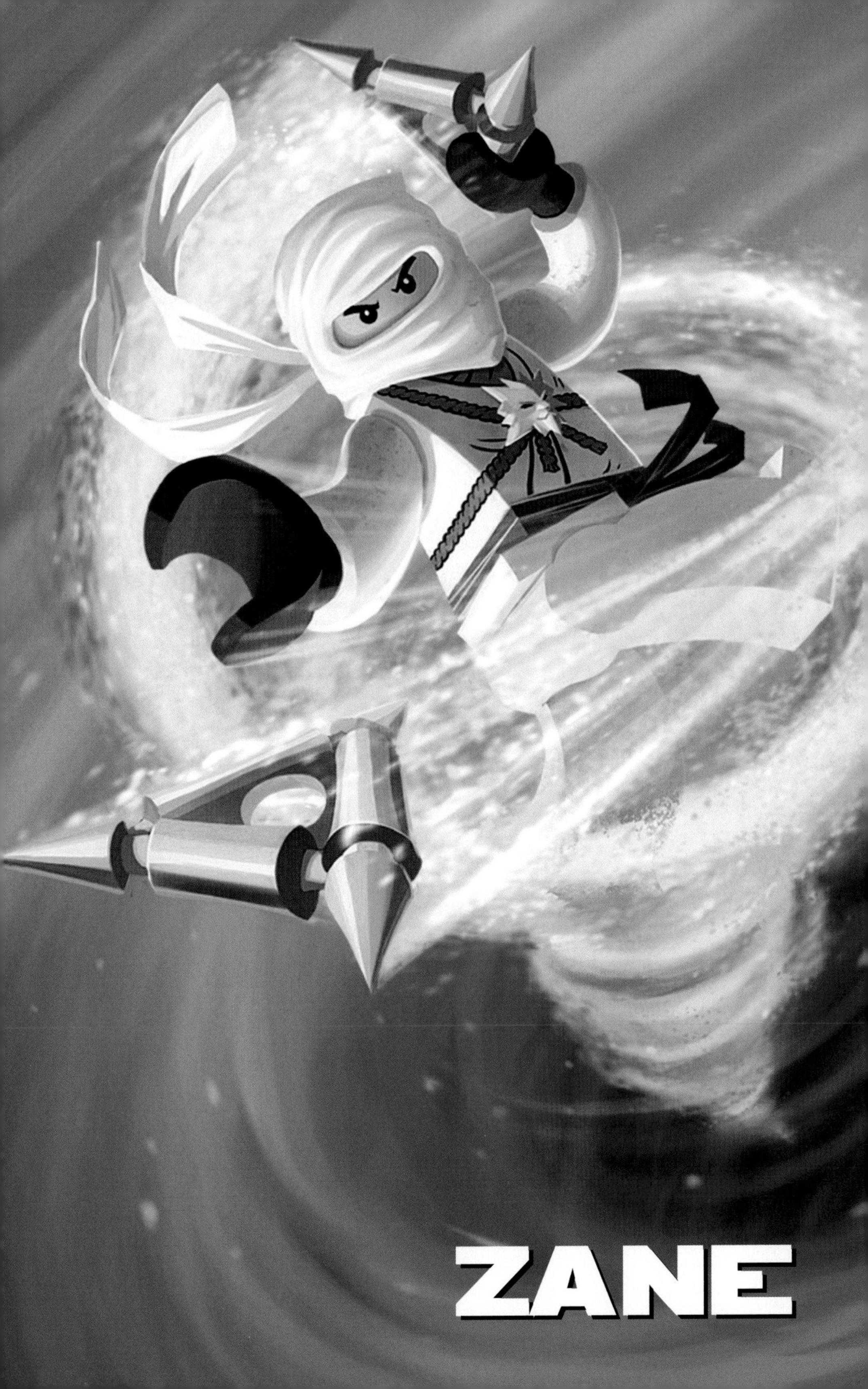
ZANE

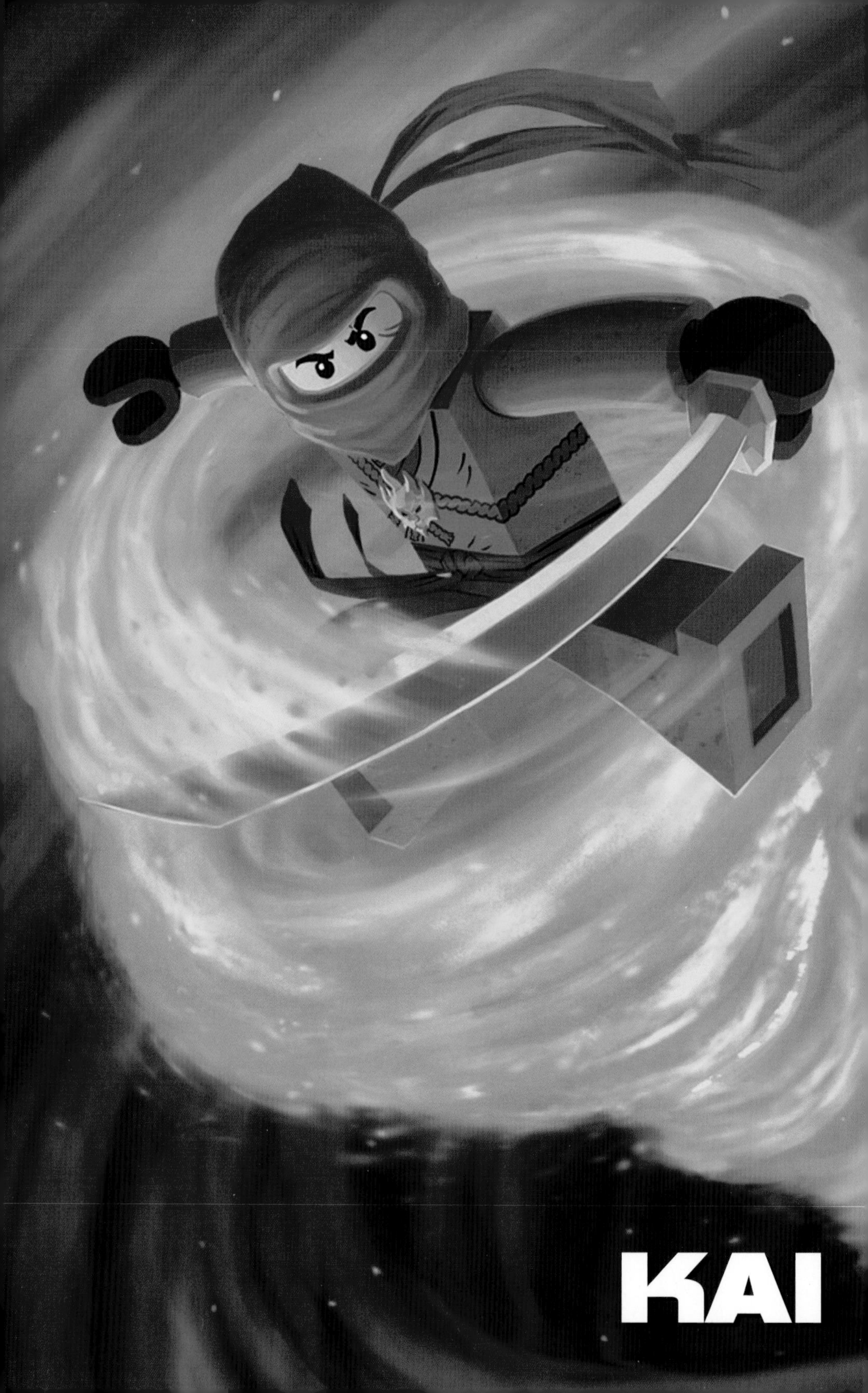
KAI

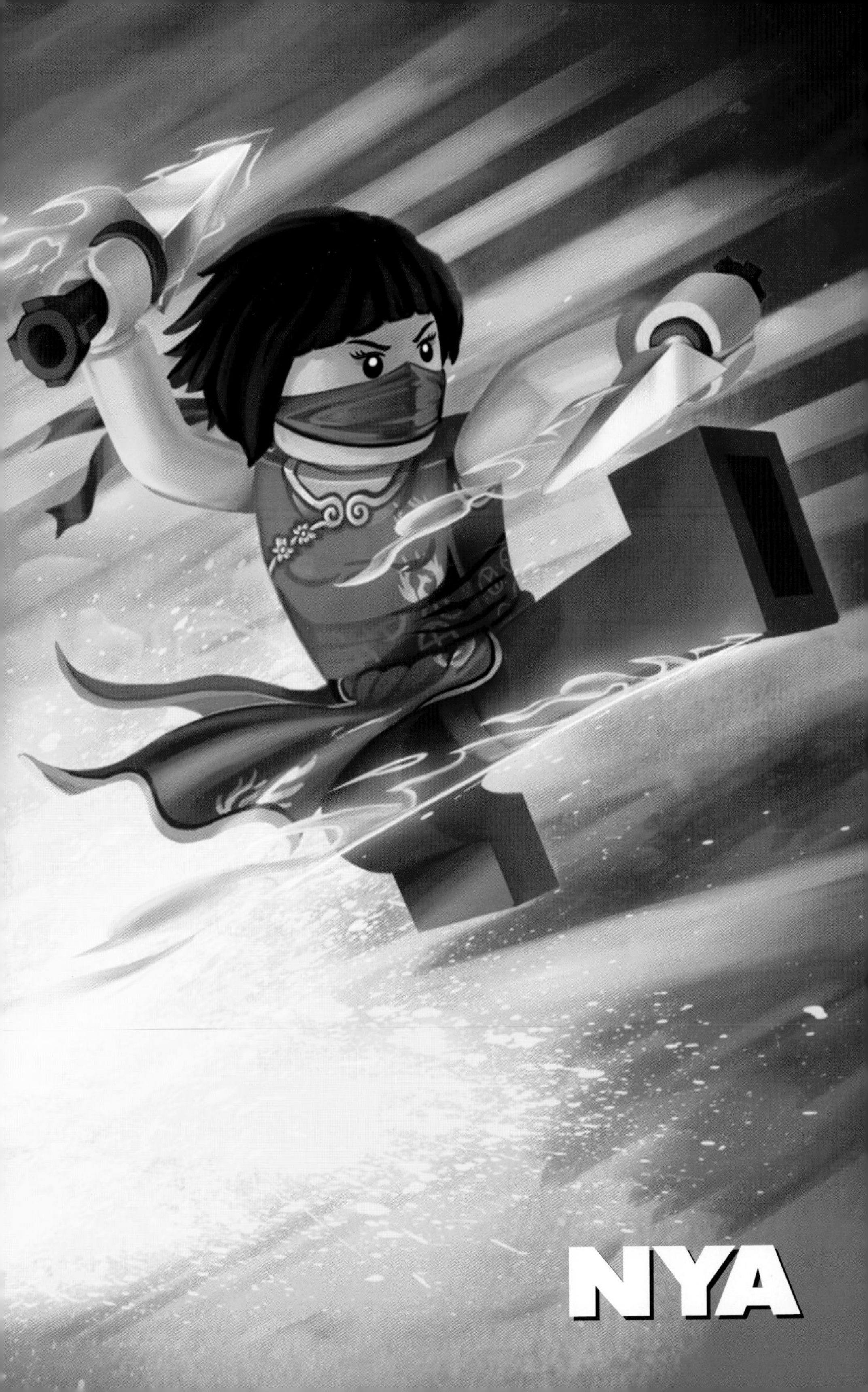
NYA

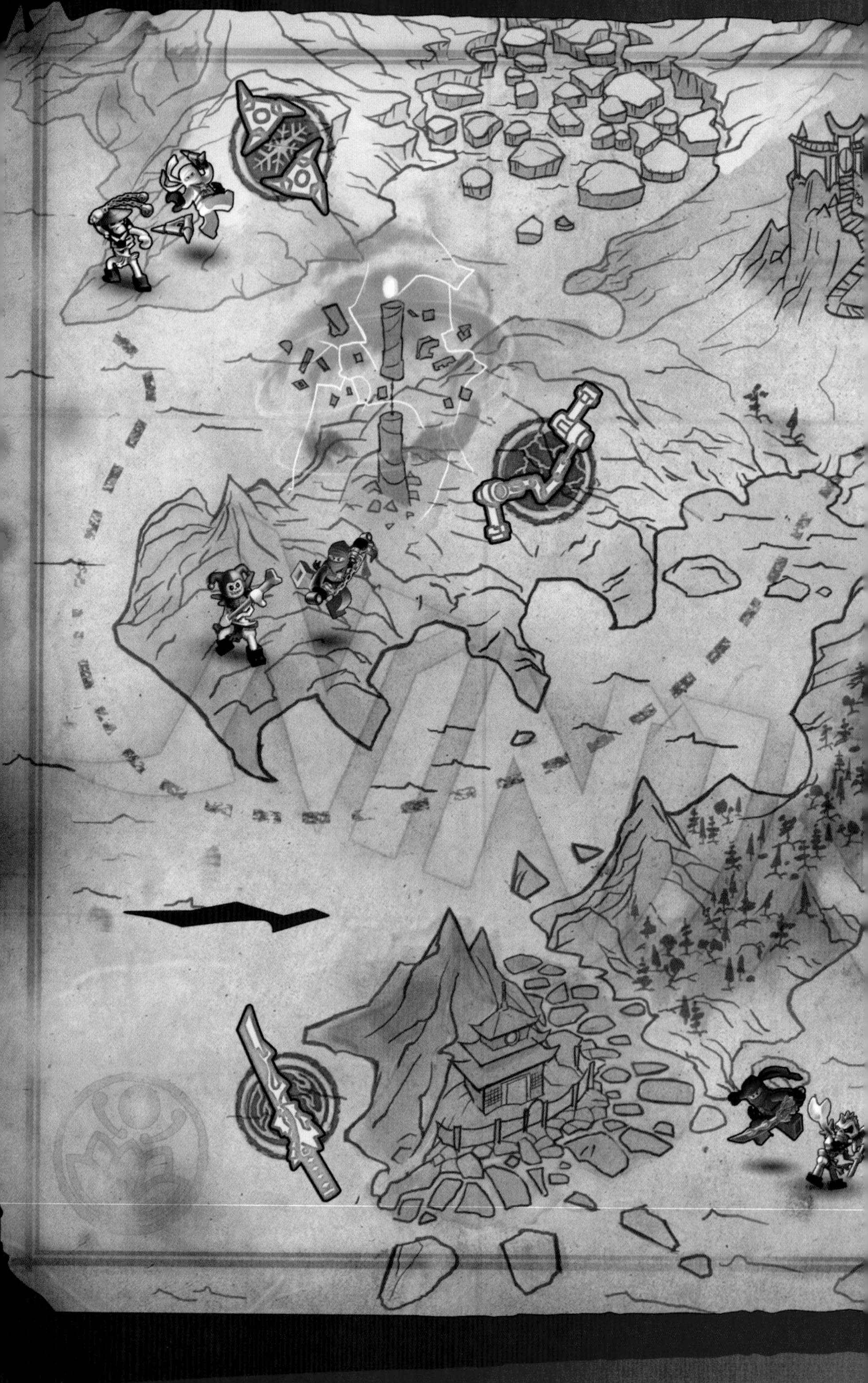

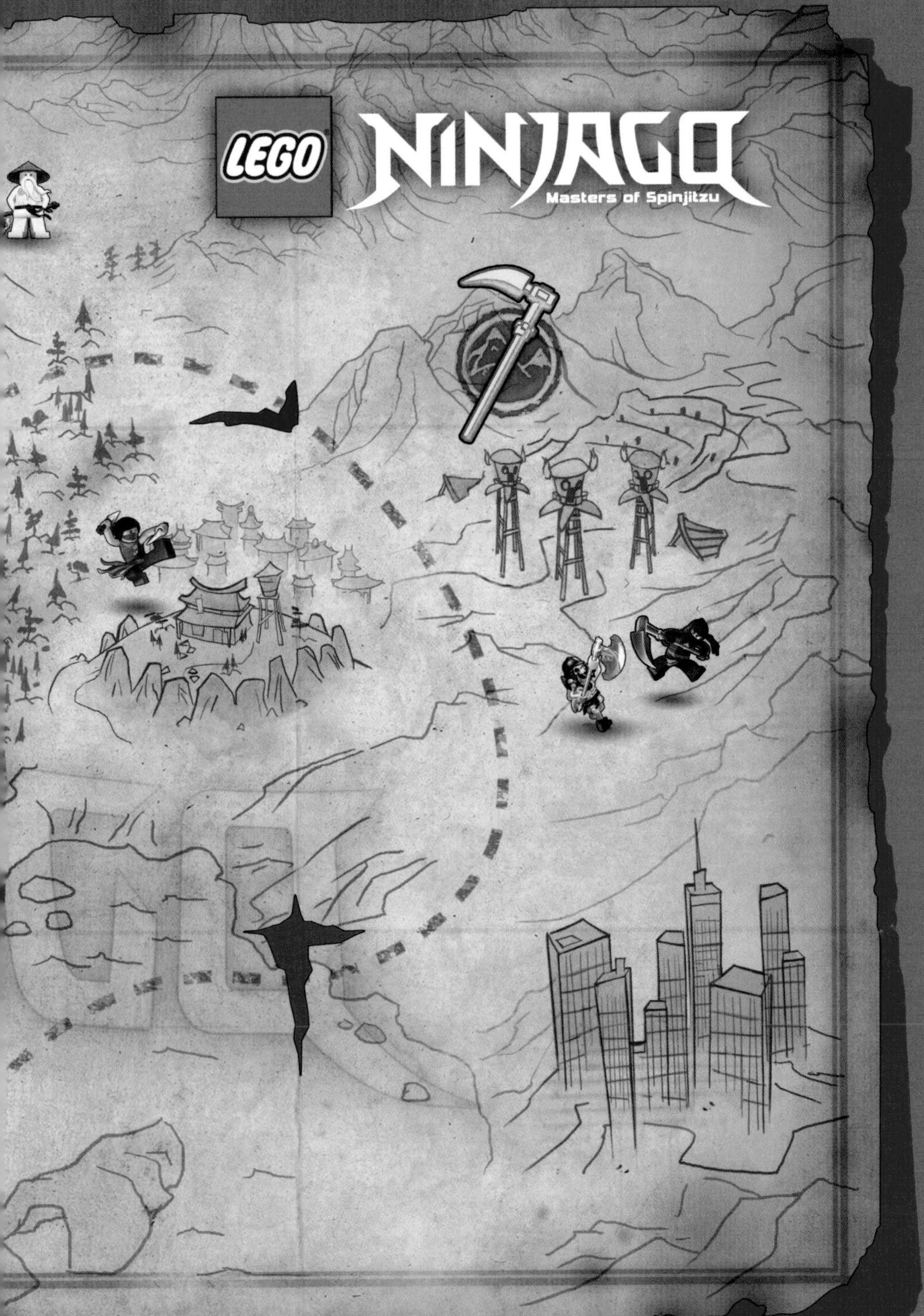
LEGO
NINJAGO
Masters of Spinjitzu

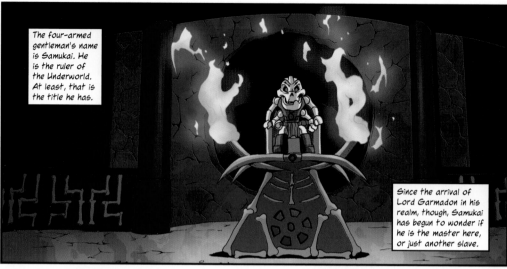

The four-armed gentleman's name is Samukai. He is the ruler of the Underworld. At least, that is the title he has.

Since the arrival of Lord Garmadon in his realm, though, Samukai has begun to wonder if he is the master here, or just another slave.

BLAST GARMADON AND HIS PLANS!

MY SKELETON ARMY COULD HAVE CONQUERED NINJAGO BY NOW IF NOT FOR HIS DELAYS.

OH, REALLY, SAMUKAI? TELL ME MORE.

GARMADON! I WISH YOU WOULD STOP SNEAKING AROUND LIKE THAT!

SMASH

IT'S A HOBBY.

NOW WHAT IS ALL THIS ABOUT MY GETTING IN THE WAY OF YOUR CONQUEST OF NINJAGO?

YOU KNOW EXACTLY WHAT I AM TALKING ABOUT.

IF WE ELIMINATE SENSEI WU AND HIS FOUR YOUNG NINJA, THERE WOULD BE NO ONE TO STAND AGAINST US.

AND YOU THINK *YOU* CAN DEFEAT THEM? I'LL TELL YOU WHAT, THEN...

THE WAGER, PART ONE

GREG FARSHTEY -- HONORABLE WRITER
PAULO HENRIQUE -- AUGUST ARTIST
LAURIE E. SMITH -- HUMBLE COLORIST
BRYAN SENKA -- LOYAL LETTERER
MICHAEL PETRANEK -- EDITORIAL STUDENT
JIM SALICRUP -- EDITORIAL MASTER

LET GO OF ME! WHAT SORT OF WAGER DID YOU HAVE IN MIND?

ONE YOU ARE CERTAIN TO LIKE. WIN, AND YOU GET EVERYTHING YOU HAVE EVER WANTED...

AND IF I LOSE?

SURELY YOU DON'T ADMIT TO THAT POSSIBILITY?

AH, BUT YOU DID LOSE ONCE BEFORE, DIDN'T YOU?

"YOU KNOW THAT WHEN I WAS FIRST EXILED HERE, SO LONG AGO," SAYS GARMADON...

"YOU WANTED ME TO BE ONE MORE OF YOUR SOLDIERS. I SAID NO, AND WE FOUGHT TO SETTLE MATTERS."

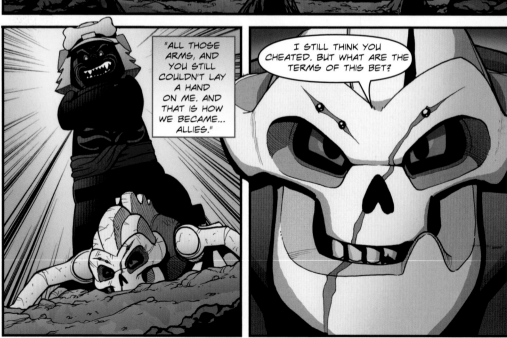

"ALL THOSE ARMS, AND YOU STILL COULDN'T LAY A HAND ON ME. AND THAT IS HOW WE BECAME... ALLIES."

I STILL THINK YOU CHEATED. BUT WHAT ARE THE TERMS OF THIS BET?

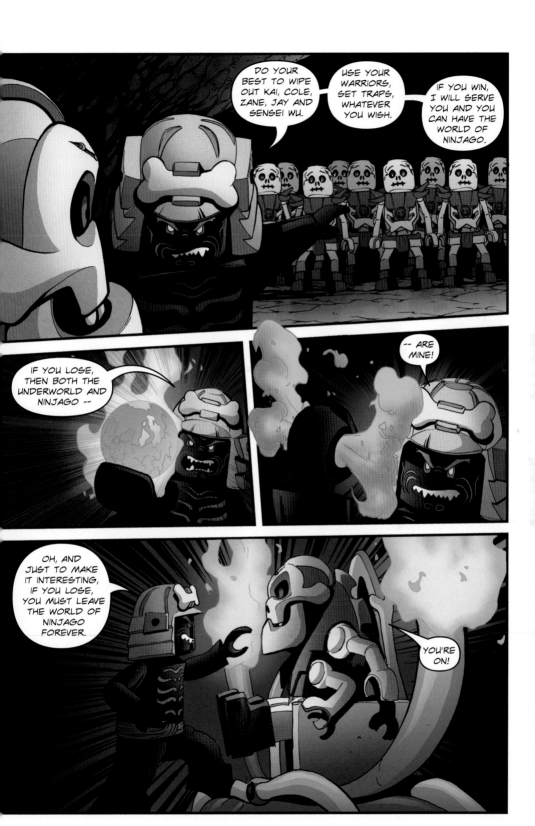

KRUNCHA! NUCKAL! KRAZI!

WHERE ARE YOU BONEHEADS? WE HAVE A JOB TO DO.

SAMUKAI IS SO PREDICTABLE.

WHILE HE CHASES AFTER SENSEI WU AND HIS TEAM, HE HAS NO IDEA WHAT I'M REALLY AFTER. BUT HE'LL LEARN.

GARMADON IS A FOOL. HE THINKS I DON'T KNOW THERE IS MORE TO THIS WAGER THAN WHAT HE HAS SAID.

BUT I WILL DEFEAT THE SENSEI AND HIS TEAM OF CHILDREN, AND THEN GARMADON AS WELL.

THIS WAGER IS AS GOOD AS WON.

"NOT EVEN THE FOUR NINJA CAN STOP ME NOW!"

And so it begins ..

ORIGINS

Gamblin' Greg Farshtey — Writer • Poker-faced Paulo Henrique — Artist

Laurie "Let-it-ride" E. Smith — Colorist • Bettin' Bryan Senka — Letterer

Michael "The Player" Petranek — Associate Editor • Jim "Jackpot" Salicrup — Editor-in-Chief

TO WIN MY WAGER WITH GARMADON, I MUST DESTROY THESE FOUR NINJA.

AND TO DO THAT, I NEED KNOWLEDGE... I MUST KNOW ALL I CAN OF HOW SENSEI WU'S TEAM CAME TO BE.

"IT TRULY BEGAN," SAYS SAMUKAI, "MANY, MANY THOUSANDS OF YEARS AGO, WHEN THE FATHER OF SENSEI WU AND GARMADON CREATED FOUR GOLDEN WEAPONS.

"SEPARATELY, THESE WEAPONS WERE INCREDIBLY POWERFUL. TOGETHER, THEIR MIGHT WOULD BE DEVASTATING.

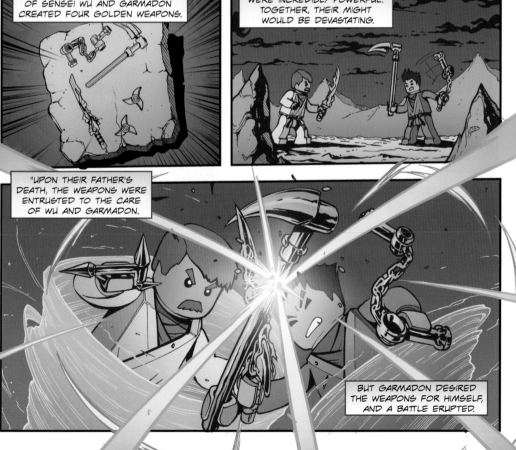

"UPON THEIR FATHER'S DEATH, THE WEAPONS WERE ENTRUSTED TO THE CARE OF WU AND GARMADON.

BUT GARMADON DESIRED THE WEAPONS FOR HIMSELF, AND A BATTLE ERUPTED.

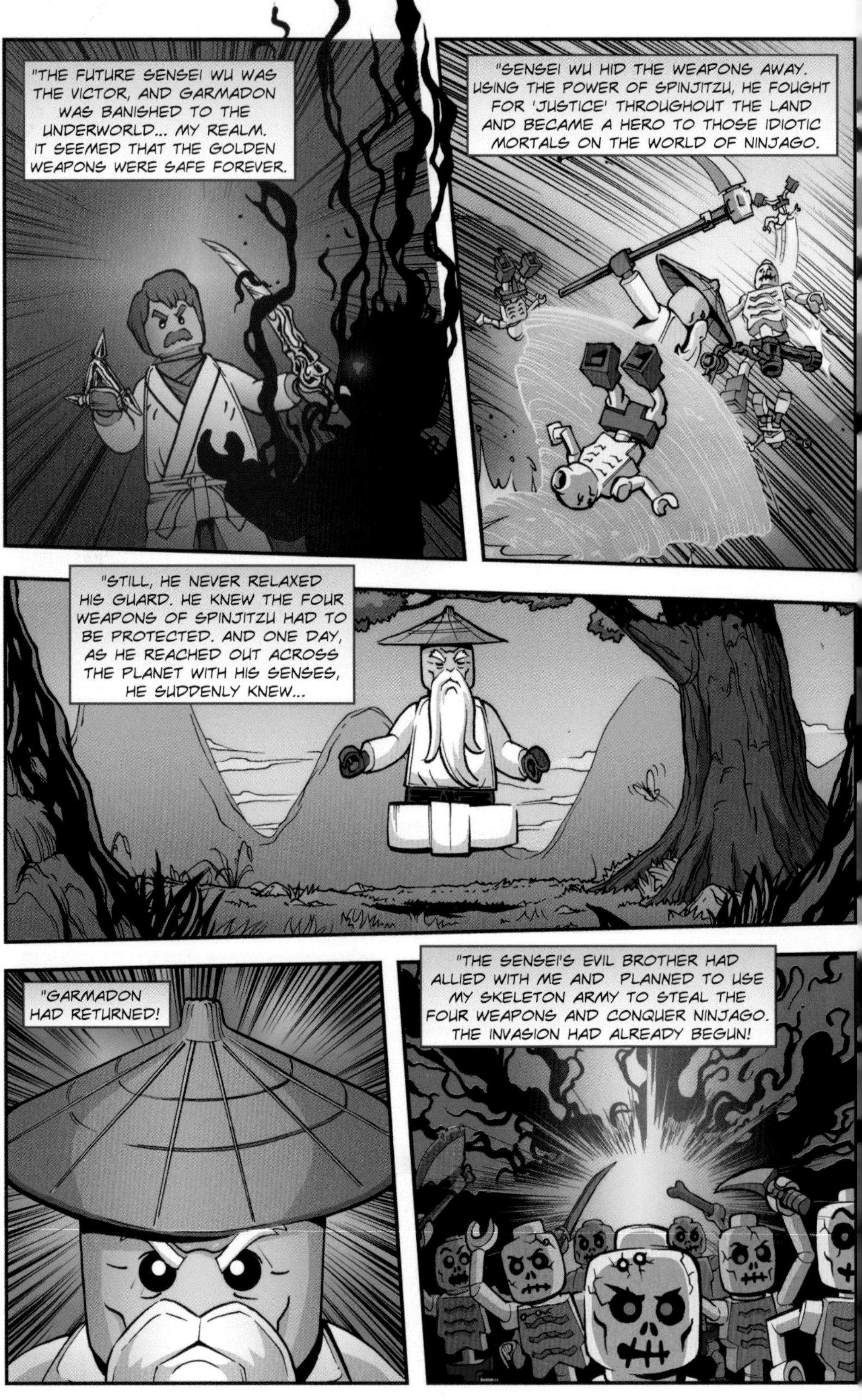
"THE FUTURE SENSEI WU WAS THE VICTOR, AND GARMADON WAS BANISHED TO THE UNDERWORLD... MY REALM. IT SEEMED THAT THE GOLDEN WEAPONS WERE SAFE FOREVER.
"SENSEI WU HID THE WEAPONS AWAY. USING THE POWER OF SPINJITZU, HE FOUGHT FOR 'JUSTICE' THROUGHOUT THE LAND AND BECAME A HERO TO THOSE IDIOTIC MORTALS ON THE WORLD OF NINJAGO.
"STILL, HE NEVER RELAXED HIS GUARD. HE KNEW THE FOUR WEAPONS OF SPINJITZU HAD TO BE PROTECTED. AND ONE DAY, AS HE REACHED OUT ACROSS THE PLANET WITH HIS SENSES, HE SUDDENLY KNEW...
"GARMADON HAD RETURNED!
"THE SENSEI'S EVIL BROTHER HAD ALLIED WITH ME AND PLANNED TO USE MY SKELETON ARMY TO STEAL THE FOUR WEAPONS AND CONQUER NINJAGO. THE INVASION HAD ALREADY BEGUN!

"SENSEI WU TRIED TO STOP MY WARRIORS, BUT EVEN HE KNEW HE COULD NOT BE EVERYWHERE AT ONCE. HE NEEDED HELP."

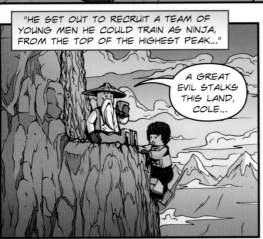

"HE SET OUT TO RECRUIT A TEAM OF YOUNG MEN HE COULD TRAIN AS NINJA, FROM THE TOP OF THE HIGHEST PEAK..."

A GREAT EVIL STALKS THIS LAND, COLE...

"TO THE BOTTOM OF A FROZEN LAKE..."

IF MY BROTHER SEIZES CONTROL OF THE FOUR WEAPONS OF SPINJITZU, OUR WORLD IS DOOMED, ZANE...

"AND EVERYWHERE IN BETWEEN."

THAT IS WHY I NEED YOUR HELP, JAY. WILL YOU AID ME?

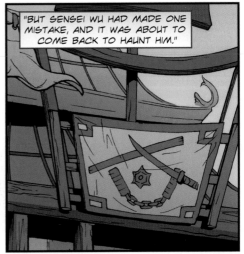

"BUT SENSEI WU HAD MADE ONE MISTAKE, AND IT WAS ABOUT TO COME BACK TO HAUNT HIM."

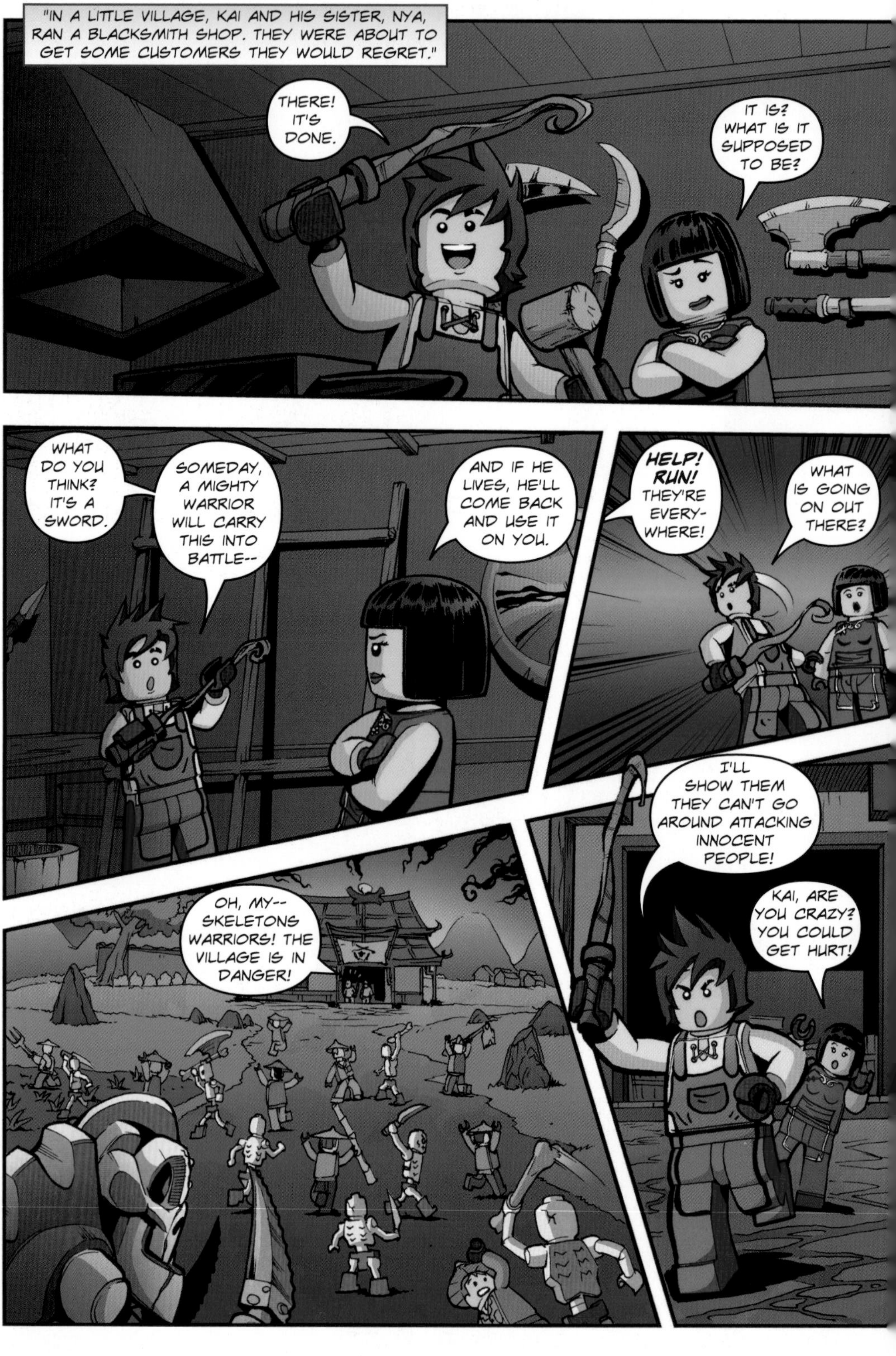
"IN A LITTLE VILLAGE, KAI AND HIS SISTER, NYA, RAN A BLACKSMITH SHOP. THEY WERE ABOUT TO GET SOME CUSTOMERS THEY WOULD REGRET."
THERE! IT'S DONE.
IT IS? WHAT IS IT SUPPOSED TO BE?
WHAT DO YOU THINK? IT'S A SWORD.
SOMEDAY, A MIGHTY WARRIOR WILL CARRY THIS INTO BATTLE--
AND IF HE LIVES, HE'LL COME BACK AND USE IT ON YOU.
HELP! RUN! THEY'RE EVERY-WHERE!
WHAT IS GOING ON OUT THERE?
OH, MY-- SKELETONS WARRIORS! THE VILLAGE IS IN DANGER!
I'LL SHOW THEM THEY CAN'T GO AROUND ATTACKING INNOCENT PEOPLE!
KAI, ARE YOU CRAZY? YOU COULD GET HURT!

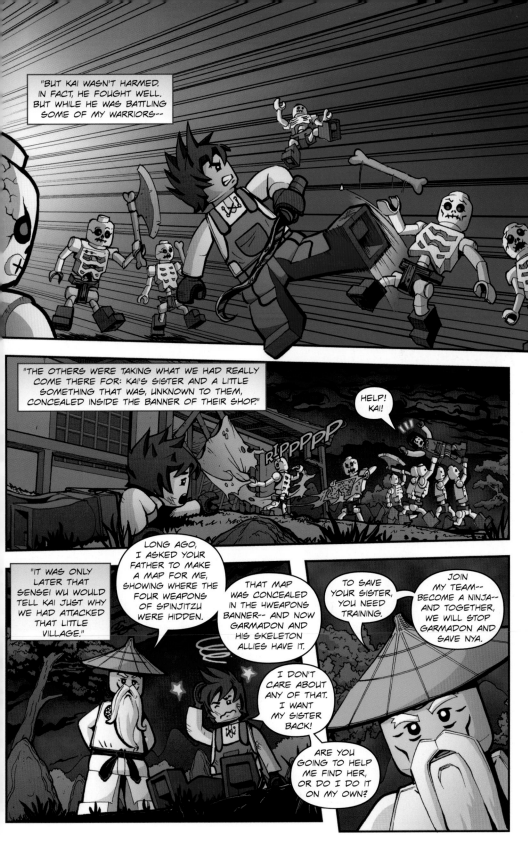

"BUT KAI WASN'T HARMED. IN FACT, HE FOUGHT WELL. BUT WHILE HE WAS BATTLING SOME OF MY WARRIORS--

"THE OTHERS WERE TAKING WHAT WE HAD REALLY COME THERE FOR: KAI'S SISTER AND A LITTLE SOMETHING THAT WAS, UNKNOWN TO THEM, CONCEALED INSIDE THE BANNER OF THEIR SHOP!"

HELP! KAI!

RIPPPPP

"IT WAS ONLY LATER THAT SENSEI WU WOULD TELL KAI JUST WHY WE HAD ATTACKED THAT LITTLE VILLAGE."

LONG AGO, I ASKED YOUR FATHER TO MAKE A MAP FOR ME, SHOWING WHERE THE FOUR WEAPONS OF SPINJITZU WERE HIDDEN.

THAT MAP WAS CONCEALED IN THE 4WEAPONS BANNER-- AND NOW GARMADON AND HIS SKELETON ALLIES HAVE IT.

TO SAVE YOUR SISTER, YOU NEED TRAINING.

JOIN MY TEAM-- BECOME A NINJA-- AND TOGETHER, WE WILL STOP GARMADON AND SAVE NYA.

I DON'T CARE ABOUT ANY OF THAT. I WANT MY SISTER BACK!

ARE YOU GOING TO HELP ME FIND HER, OR DO I DO IT ON MY OWN?

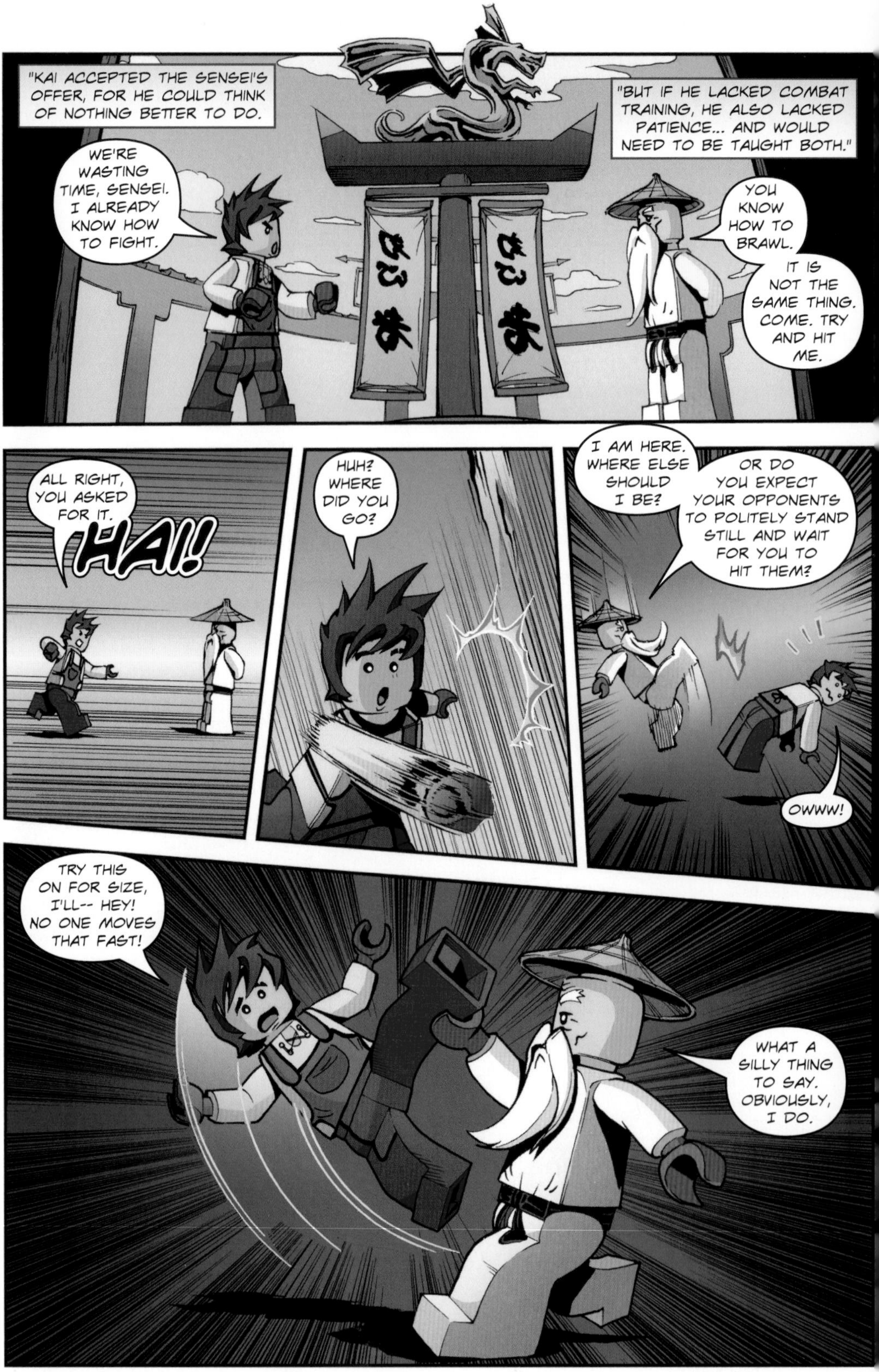
"KAI ACCEPTED THE SENSEI'S OFFER, FOR HE COULD THINK OF NOTHING BETTER TO DO.
"BUT IF HE LACKED COMBAT TRAINING, HE ALSO LACKED PATIENCE... AND WOULD NEED TO BE TAUGHT BOTH."
WE'RE WASTING TIME, SENSEI. I ALREADY KNOW HOW TO FIGHT.
YOU KNOW HOW TO BRAWL.
IT IS NOT THE SAME THING. COME. TRY AND HIT ME.
ALL RIGHT, YOU ASKED FOR IT.
HAI!
HUH? WHERE DID YOU GO?
I AM HERE. WHERE ELSE SHOULD I BE?
OR DO YOU EXPECT YOUR OPPONENTS TO POLITELY STAND STILL AND WAIT FOR YOU TO HIT THEM?
OWWW!
TRY THIS ON FOR SIZE, I'LL-- HEY! NO ONE MOVES THAT FAST!
WHAT A SILLY THING TO SAY. OBVIOUSLY, I DO.

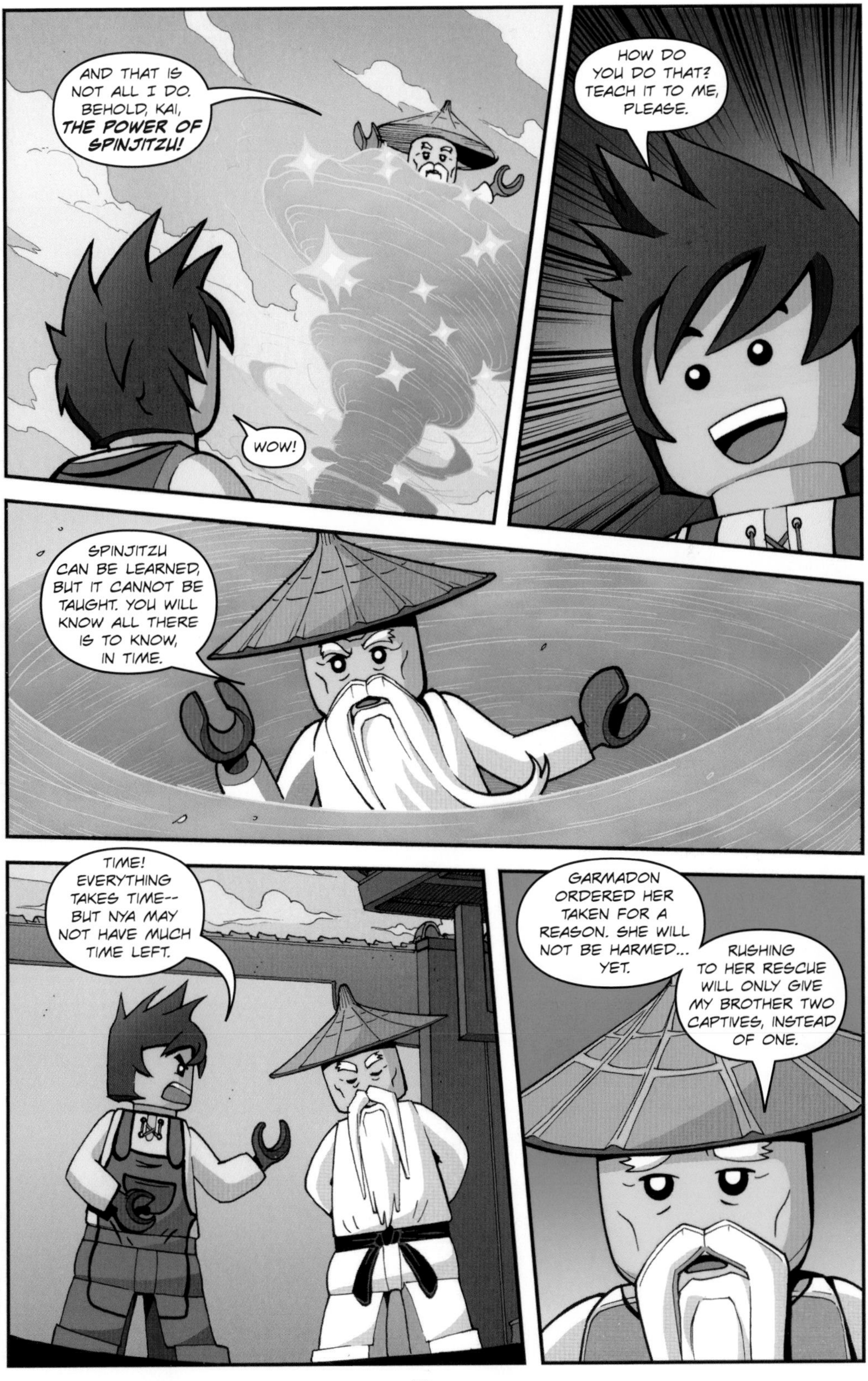
AND THAT IS NOT ALL I DO. BEHOLD, KAI, THE POWER OF SPINJITZU!
WOW!
HOW DO YOU DO THAT? TEACH IT TO ME, PLEASE.
SPINJITZU CAN BE LEARNED, BUT IT CANNOT BE TAUGHT. YOU WILL KNOW ALL THERE IS TO KNOW, IN TIME.
TIME! EVERYTHING TAKES TIME-- BUT NYA MAY NOT HAVE MUCH TIME LEFT.
GARMADON ORDERED HER TAKEN FOR A REASON. SHE WILL NOT BE HARMED... YET.
RUSHING TO HER RESCUE WILL ONLY GIVE MY BROTHER TWO CAPTIVES, INSTEAD OF ONE.

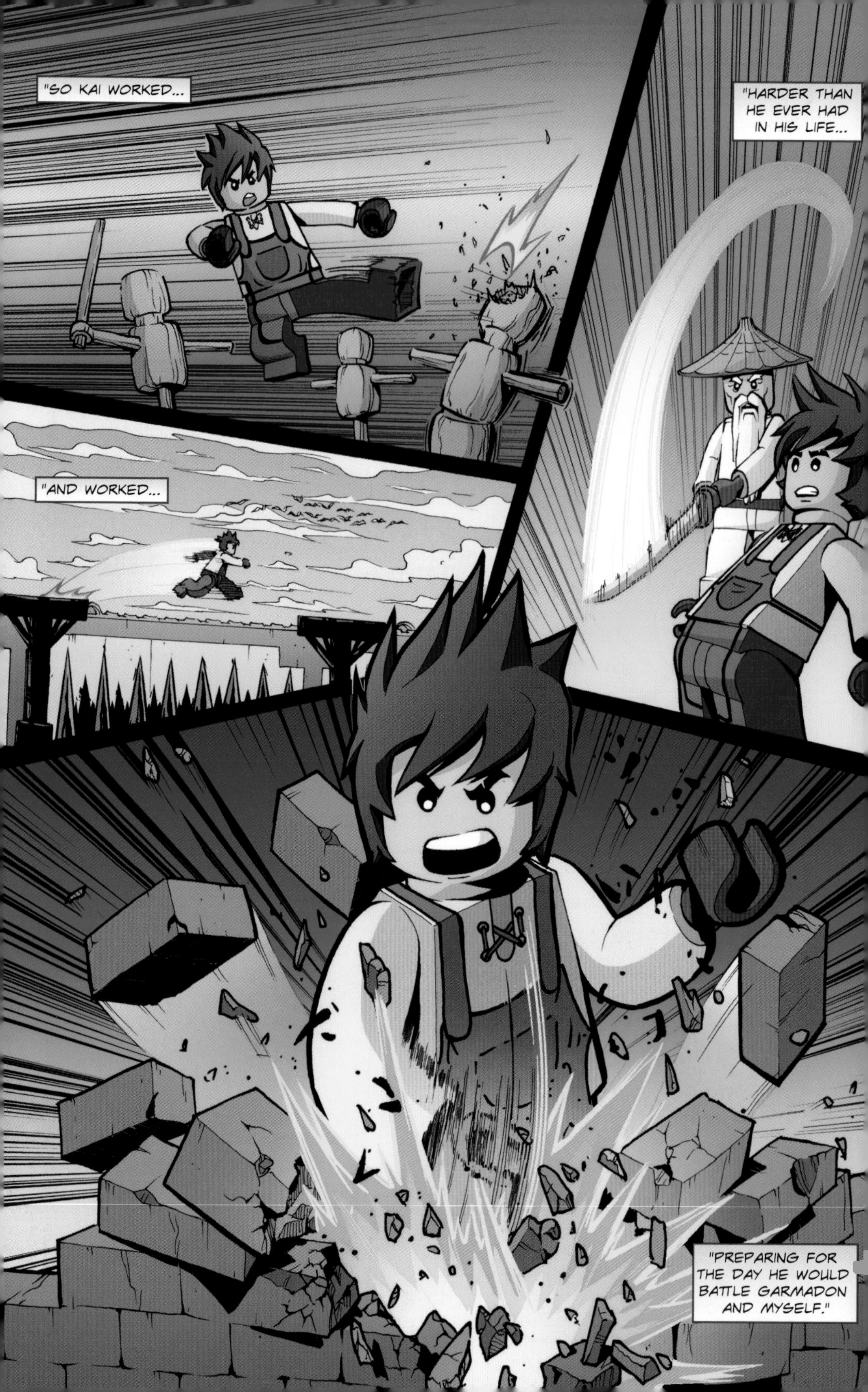
"SO KAI WORKED...
"HARDER THAN HE EVER HAD IN HIS LIFE...
"AND WORKED...
"PREPARING FOR THE DAY HE WOULD BATTLE GARMADON AND MYSELF."

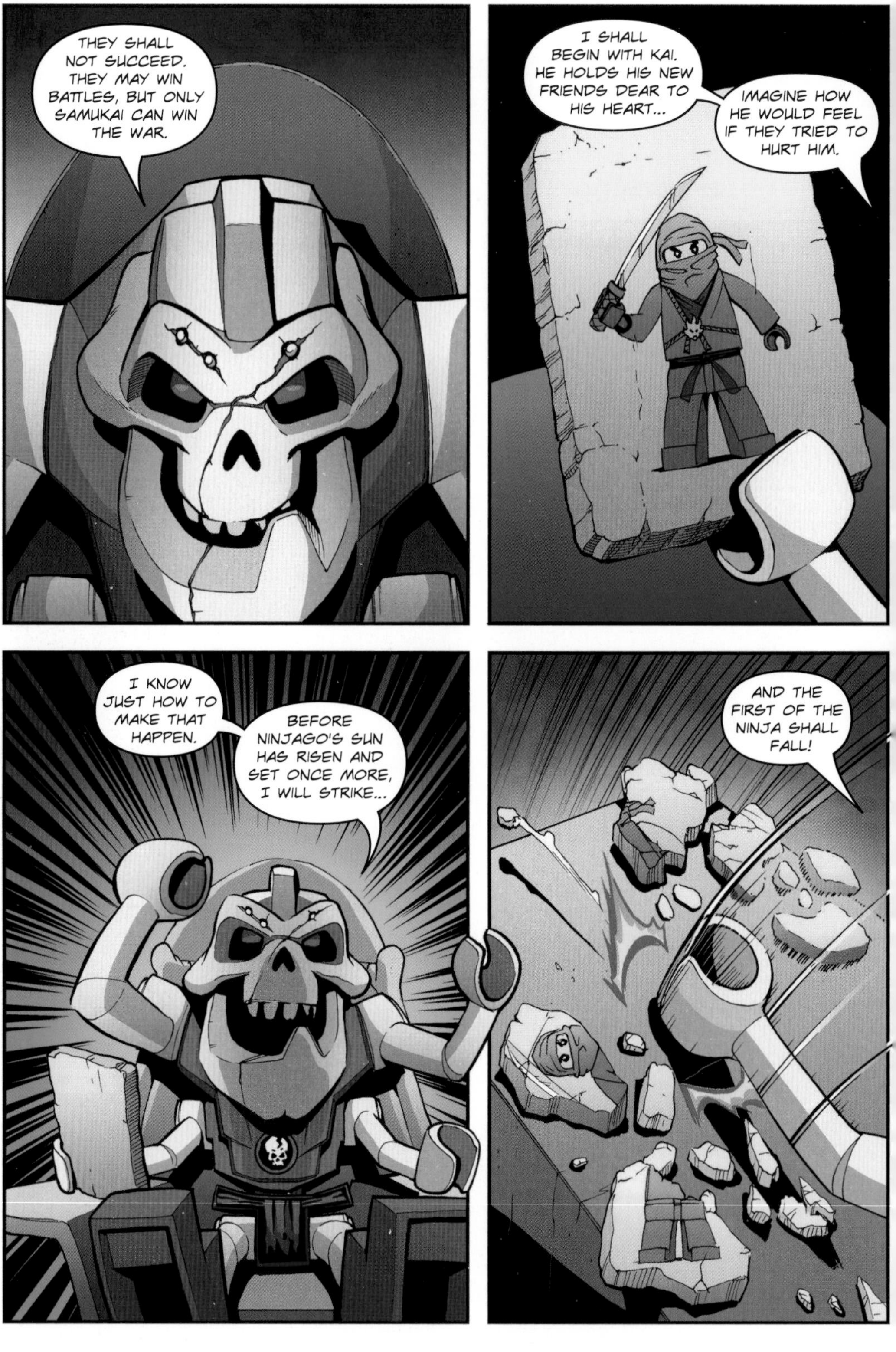
THEY SHALL NOT SUCCEED. THEY MAY WIN BATTLES, BUT ONLY SAMUKAI CAN WIN THE WAR.
I SHALL BEGIN WITH KAI. HE HOLDS HIS NEW FRIENDS DEAR TO HIS HEART...
IMAGINE HOW HE WOULD FEEL IF THEY TRIED TO HURT HIM.
I KNOW JUST HOW TO MAKE THAT HAPPEN.
BEFORE NINJAGO'S SUN HAS RISEN AND SET ONCE MORE, I WILL STRIKE...
AND THE FIRST OF THE NINJA SHALL FALL!

Not far from the temporary campsite of Sensei Wu and his four ninja...

OKAY, SO, WHEN I SEE KAI, I CHASE AFTER HIM.

NO, NUCKAL, YOU LET HIM CHASE AFTER YOU.

RIGHT, GENERAL KRUNCHA, BUT NO MATTER WHAT, DON'T LET HIM NEAR THE CRYSTAL CAVES.

NO, YOU NUMBSKULL, YOU WANT HIM TO GO INTO THE CRYSTAL CAVES! YOU'RE SUPPOSED TO LEAD HIM THERE!

HOW I'M SUPPOSED TO TRAP A NINJA WITH HELP LIKE THIS, I DON'T--

YOU WERE WRONG, GENERAL. MY SKULL'S NOT NUMB. I SURE FELT THAT!

WHACK

TURN ABOUT

"GORILLA" GREG FARSHTEY -- WRITER
"PILEDRIVER" PAULO HENRIQUE -- ARTIST
"LOCK 'N' LOAD" LAURIE E. SMITH -- COLORIST
"BAD BOY" BRYAN SENKA -- LETTERER
"MAD DOG" MICHAEL PETRANEK -- ASSOCIATE EDITOR
"JAWBREAKER" JIM SALICRUP -- EDITOR-IN-CHIEF

I'M SO DONE... AGAIN. ALL RIGHT, NUCKAL, LET'S GO OVER IT ONE MORE TIME.

28

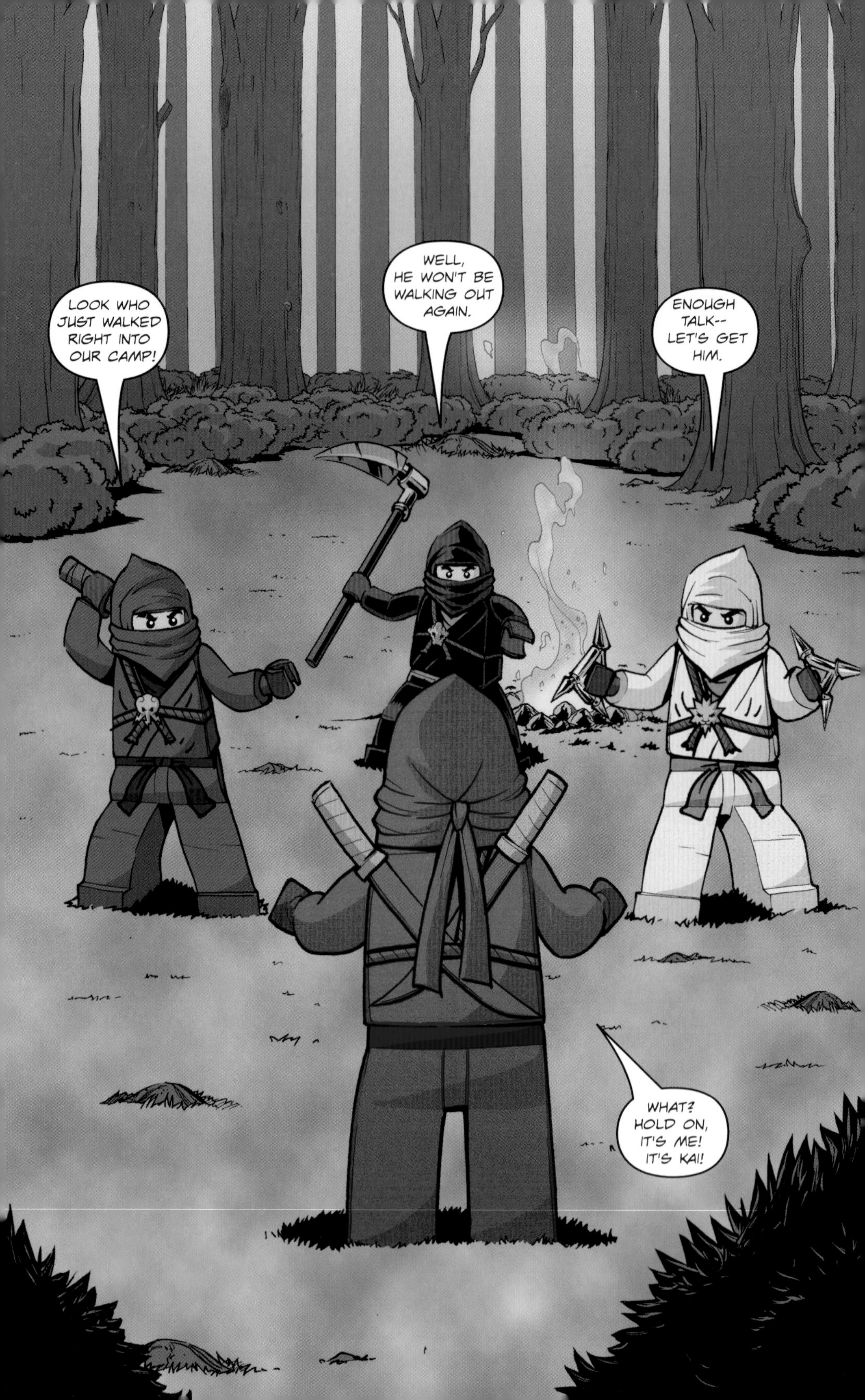
LOOK WHO JUST WALKED RIGHT INTO OUR CAMP!
WELL, HE WON'T BE WALKING OUT AGAIN.
ENOUGH TALK-- LET'S GET HIM.
WHAT? HOLD ON, IT'S ME! IT'S KAI!

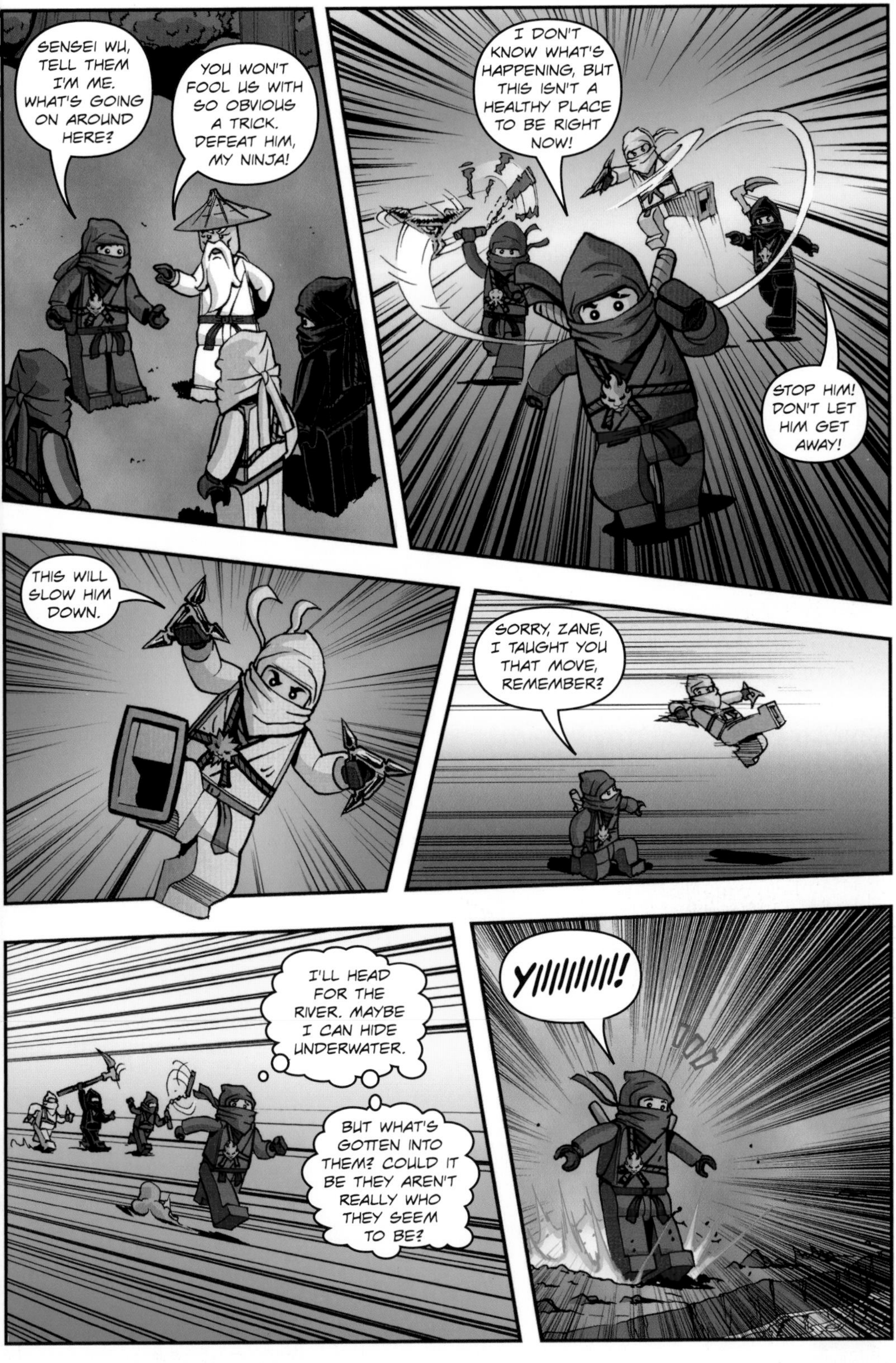
SENSEI WU, TELL THEM I'M ME. WHAT'S GOING ON AROUND HERE?
YOU WON'T FOOL US WITH SO OBVIOUS A TRICK. DEFEAT HIM, MY NINJA!
I DON'T KNOW WHAT'S HAPPENING, BUT THIS ISN'T A HEALTHY PLACE TO BE RIGHT NOW!
STOP HIM! DON'T LET HIM GET AWAY!
THIS WILL SLOW HIM DOWN.
SORRY, ZANE, I TAUGHT YOU THAT MOVE, REMEMBER?
I'LL HEAD FOR THE RIVER. MAYBE I CAN HIDE UNDERWATER.
BUT WHAT'S GOTTEN INTO THEM? COULD IT BE THEY AREN'T REALLY WHO THEY SEEM TO BE?
YIIIIIIIII!

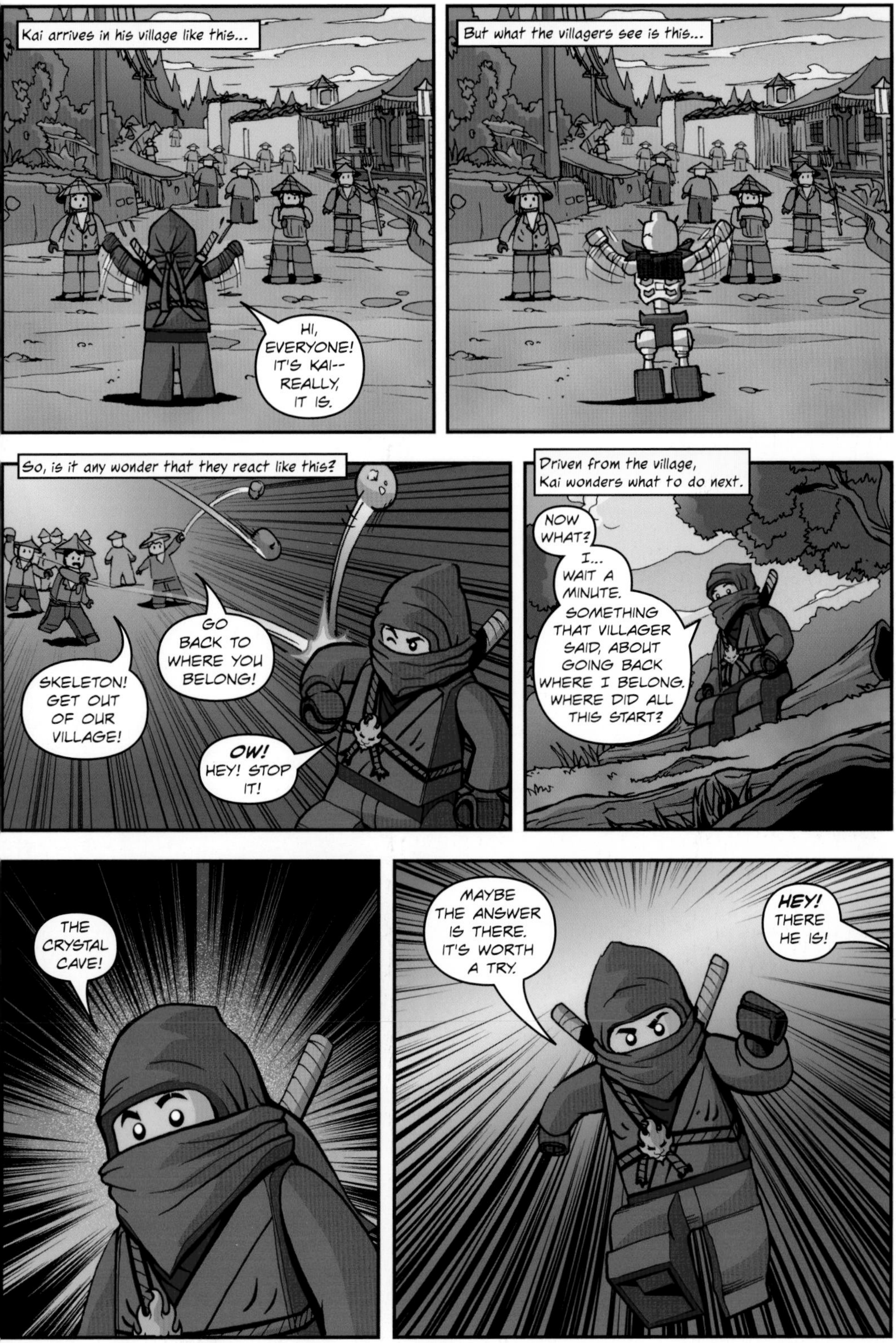
Kai arrives in his village like this...
HI, EVERYONE! IT'S KAI-- REALLY, IT IS.
But what the villagers see is this...
So, is it any wonder that they react like this?
SKELETON! GET OUT OF OUR VILLAGE!
GO BACK TO WHERE YOU BELONG!
OW! HEY! STOP IT!
Driven from the village, Kai wonders what to do next.
NOW WHAT?
I... WAIT A MINUTE. SOMETHING THAT VILLAGER SAID, ABOUT GOING BACK WHERE I BELONG. WHERE DID ALL THIS START?
THE CRYSTAL CAVE!
MAYBE THE ANSWER IS THERE. IT'S WORTH A TRY.
HEY! THERE HE IS!

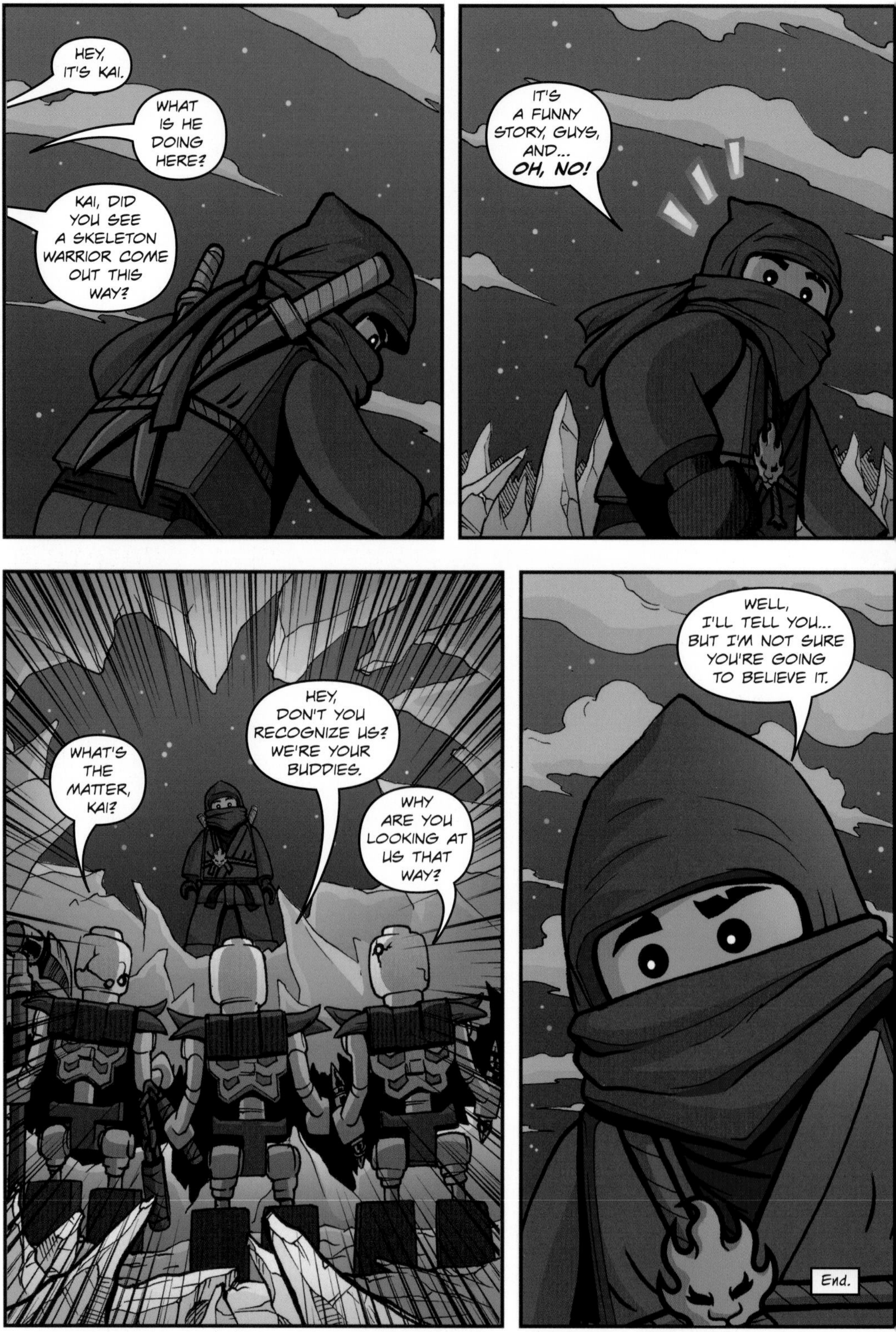
HEY, IT'S KAI.
WHAT IS HE DOING HERE?
KAI, DID YOU SEE A SKELETON WARRIOR COME OUT THIS WAY?
IT'S A FUNNY STORY, GUYS, AND... **OH, NO!**
WHAT'S THE MATTER, KAI?
HEY, DON'T YOU RECOGNIZE US? WE'RE YOUR BUDDIES.
WHY ARE YOU LOOKING AT US THAT WAY?
WELL, I'LL TELL YOU... BUT I'M NOT SURE YOU'RE GOING TO BELIEVE IT.
End.

Today.

IT'S REALLY QUITE SIMPLE, COLE...

CHOOSE A DOOR. BEHIND ONE, YOU WILL FIND YOUR FRIENDS-- BEHIND THE OTHER, CERTAIN DOOM. BUT DON'T WAIT TOO LONG...

KAI AND JAY WILL BE RUNNING OUT OF AIR BEFORE TOO LONG.

I HAVE A BETTER IDEA! I'LL *SPINJITZU* YOU AND YOUR PALS UNTIL YOU SET MY TEAMMATES FREE.

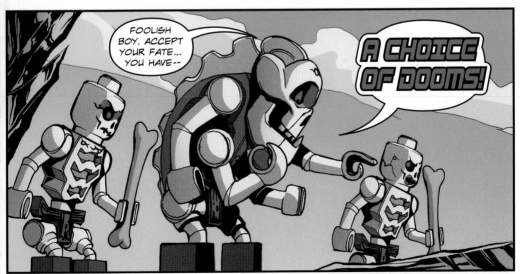

FOOLISH BOY. ACCEPT YOUR FATE... YOU HAVE--

A CHOICE OF DOOMS!

GREG FARSHTEY -- WRITER * PAULO HENRIQUE -- ARTIST * LAURIE E. SMITH -- COLORIST *
BRYAN SENKA -- LETTERER * MICHAEL PETRANEK -- ASSOCIATE EDITOR * JIM SALICRUP -- EDITOR-IN-CHIEF

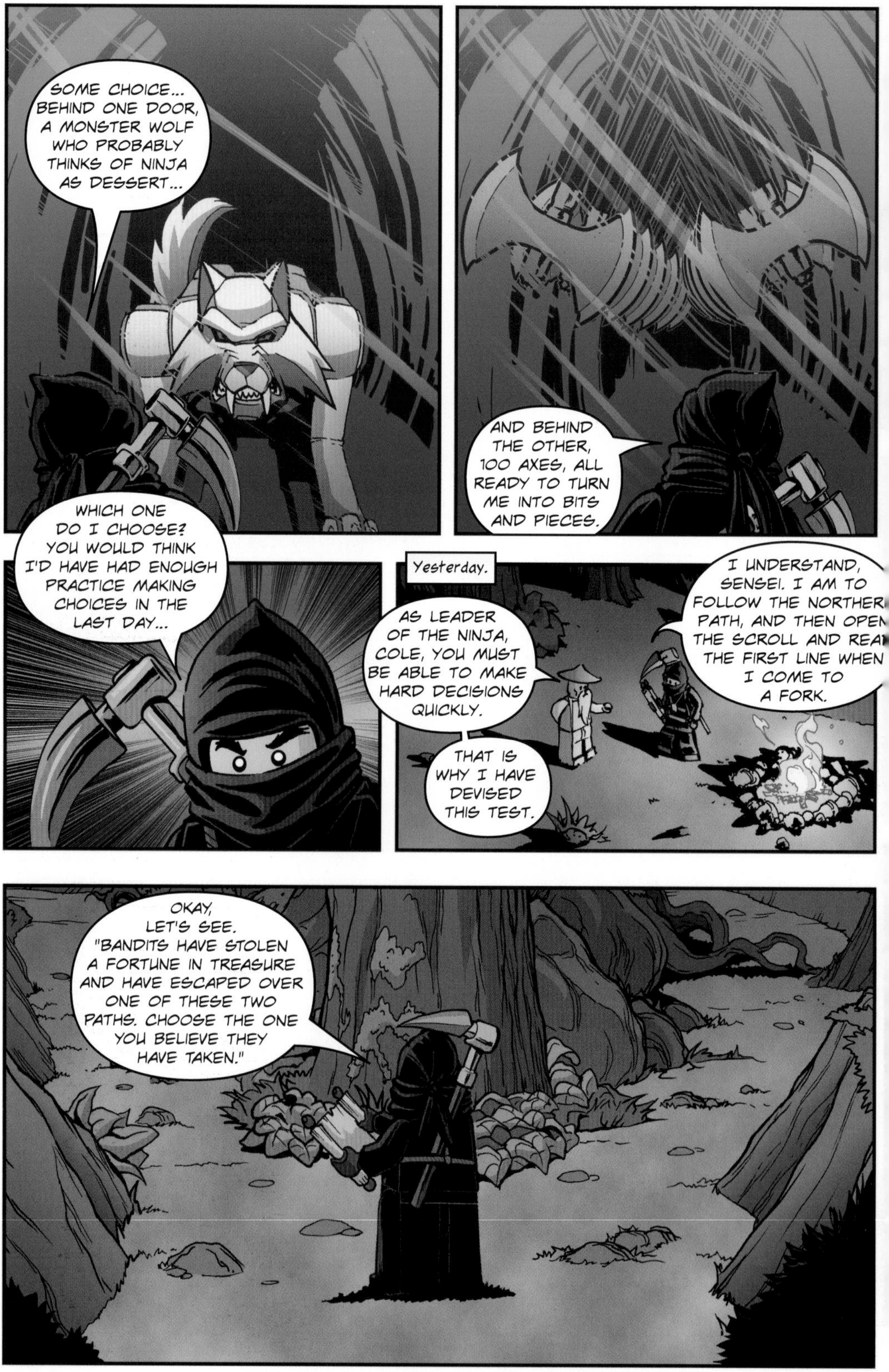
SOME CHOICE... BEHIND ONE DOOR, A MONSTER WOLF WHO PROBABLY THINKS OF NINJA AS DESSERT...
AND BEHIND THE OTHER, 100 AXES, ALL READY TO TURN ME INTO BITS AND PIECES.
WHICH ONE DO I CHOOSE? YOU WOULD THINK I'D HAVE HAD ENOUGH PRACTICE MAKING CHOICES IN THE LAST DAY...
Yesterday.
AS LEADER OF THE NINJA, COLE, YOU MUST BE ABLE TO MAKE HARD DECISIONS QUICKLY.
THAT IS WHY I HAVE DEVISED THIS TEST.
I UNDERSTAND, SENSEI. I AM TO FOLLOW THE NORTHER PATH, AND THEN OPEN THE SCROLL AND REA THE FIRST LINE WHEN I COME TO A FORK.
OKAY, LET'S SEE. "BANDITS HAVE STOLEN A FORTUNE IN TREASURE AND HAVE ESCAPED OVER ONE OF THESE TWO PATHS. CHOOSE THE ONE YOU BELIEVE THEY HAVE TAKEN."

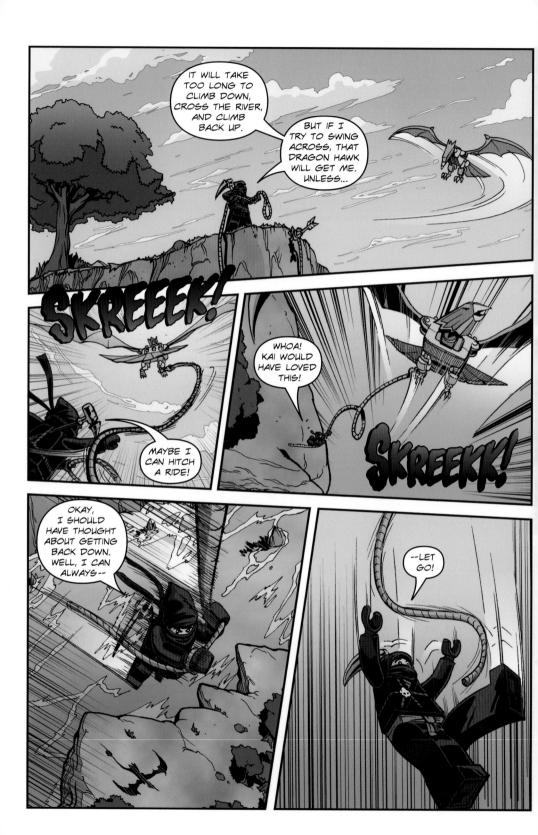

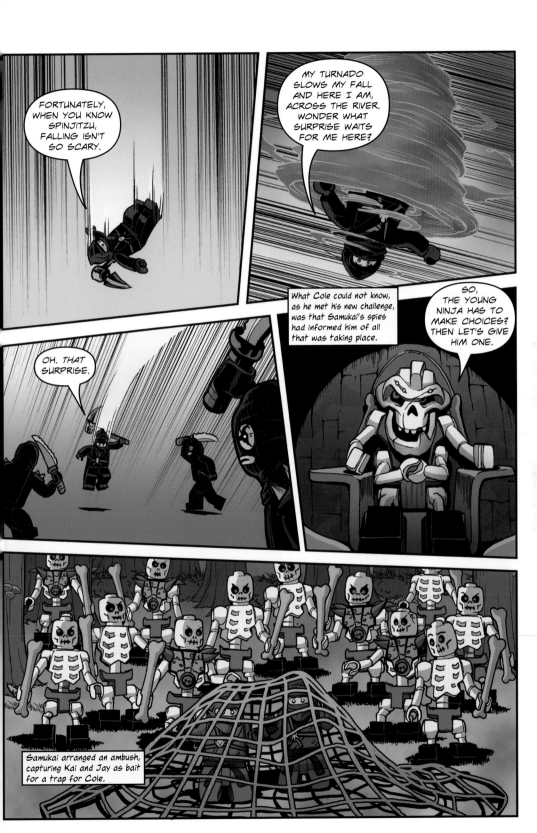

FORTUNATELY, WHEN YOU KNOW SPINJITZU, FALLING ISN'T SO SCARY.

MY TURNADO SLOWS MY FALL AND HERE I AM, ACROSS THE RIVER. WONDER WHAT SURPRISE WAITS FOR ME HERE?

What Cole could not know, as he met his new challenge, was that Samukai's spies had informed him of all that was taking place.

SO, THE YOUNG NINJA HAS TO MAKE CHOICES? THEN LET'S GIVE HIM ONE.

OH. THAT SURPRISE.

Samukai arranged an ambush, capturing Kai and Jay as bait for a trap for Cole.

"COME ALONE TO THE TWIN CAVERNS NORTHEAST OF HERE," SAMUKAI HAD SAID. "THERE YOU WILL FACE YOUR ULTIMATE CHOICE."

AND HERE I AM, NO CLOSER TO MAKING A DECISION.

COULD ONE OF THESE TRAPS BE AN ILLUSION? THEY BOTH LOOK REAL ENOUGH.

CHOOSE, NINJA! NOW!

DON'T PUSH ME!

THAT WOLF HAS TO BE REAL, DOWN TO THE FANGS AND CLAWS.

AND THOSE AXES LOOK PLENTY SHARP. THOSE FLIES HAD BETTER BE CAREFUL THEY DON'T GET SLICED, AND...

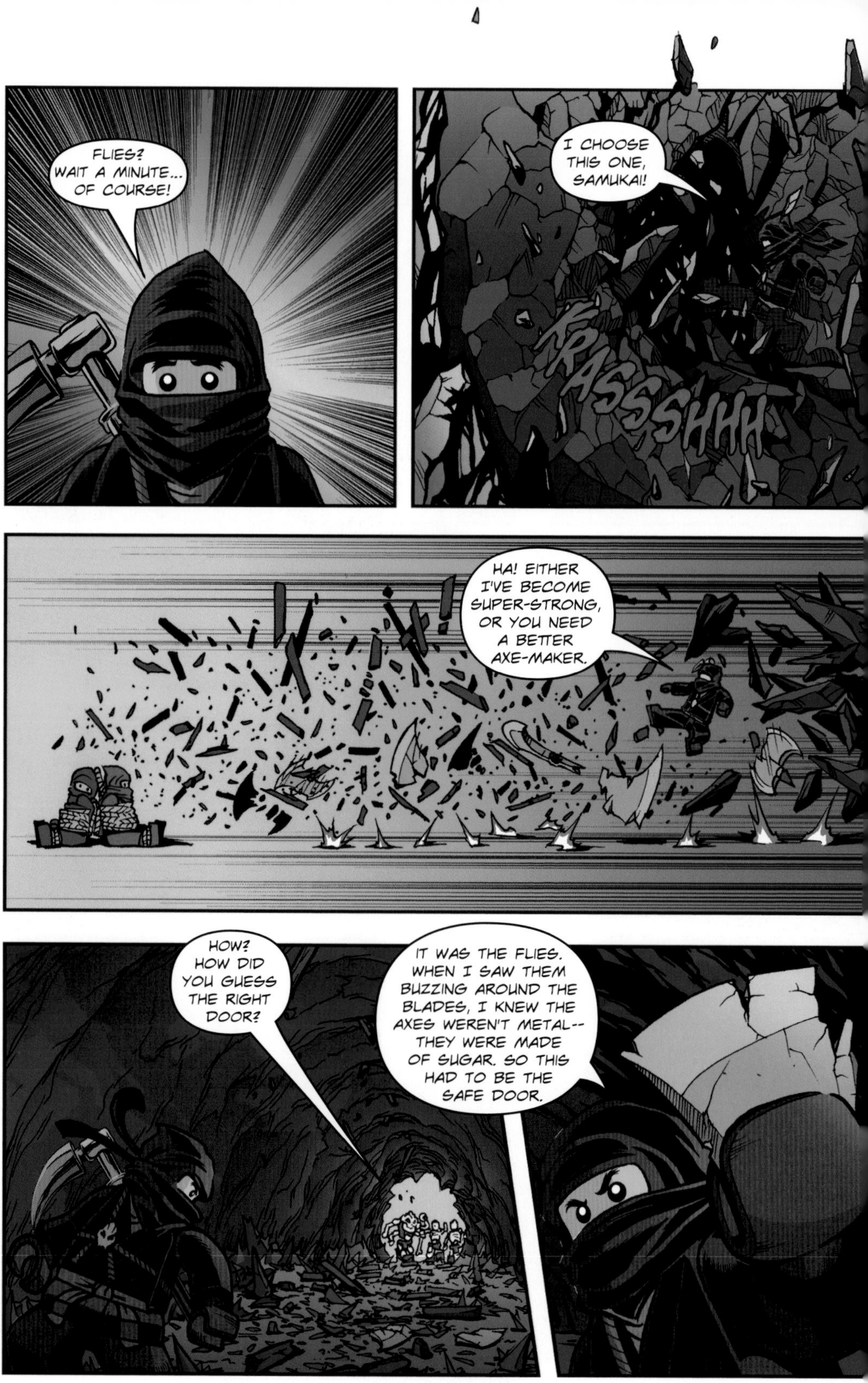
FLIES? WAIT A MINUTE... OF COURSE!
I CHOOSE THIS ONE, SAMUKAI!
KRASSSHHH
HA! EITHER I'VE BECOME SUPER-STRONG, OR YOU NEED A BETTER AXE-MAKER.
HOW? HOW DID YOU GUESS THE RIGHT DOOR?
IT WAS THE FLIES. WHEN I SAW THEM BUZZING AROUND THE BLADES, I KNEW THE AXES WEREN'T METAL-- THEY WERE MADE OF SUGAR. SO THIS HAD TO BE THE SAFE DOOR.

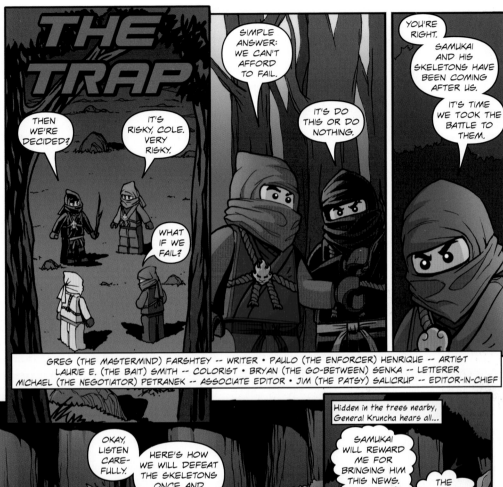

THE TRAP

THEN WE'RE DECIDED?

IT'S RISKY, COLE. VERY RISKY.

WHAT IF WE FAIL?

SIMPLE ANSWER: WE CAN'T AFFORD TO FAIL.

IT'S DO THIS OR DO NOTHING.

YOU'RE RIGHT.

SAMUKAI AND HIS SKELETONS HAVE BEEN COMING AFTER US.

IT'S TIME WE TOOK THE BATTLE TO THEM.

GREG (THE MASTERMIND) FARSHTEY -- WRITER • PAULO (THE ENFORCER) HENRIQUE -- ARTIST
LAURIE E. (THE BAIT) SMITH -- COLORIST • BRYAN (THE GO-BETWEEN) SENKA -- LETTERER
MICHAEL (THE NEGOTIATOR) PETRANEK -- ASSOCIATE EDITOR • JIM (THE PATSY) SALICRUP -- EDITOR-IN-CHIEF

OKAY, LISTEN CAREFULLY.

HERE'S HOW WE WILL DEFEAT THE SKELETONS ONCE AND FOR ALL.

Hidden in the trees nearby, General Kruncha hears all...

SAMUKAI WILL REWARD ME FOR BRINGING HIM THIS NEWS.

THE NINJA ARE PLANNING THEIR OWN DOOM!

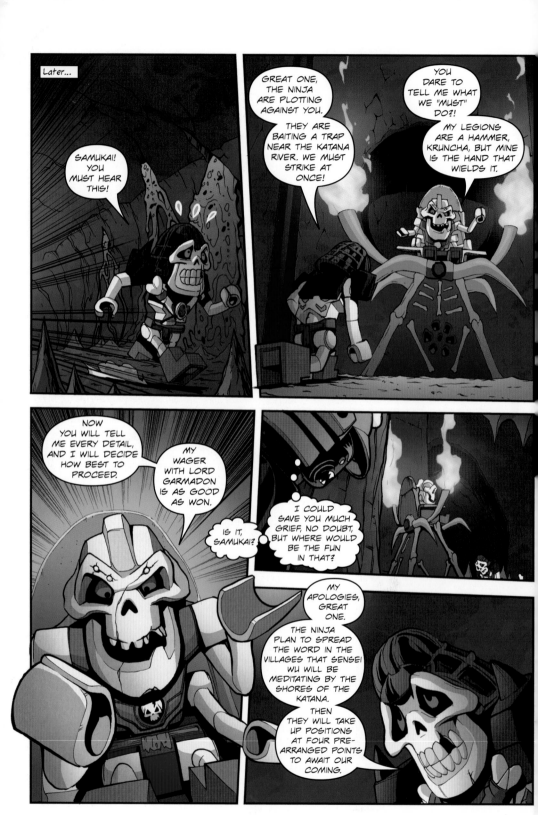

49

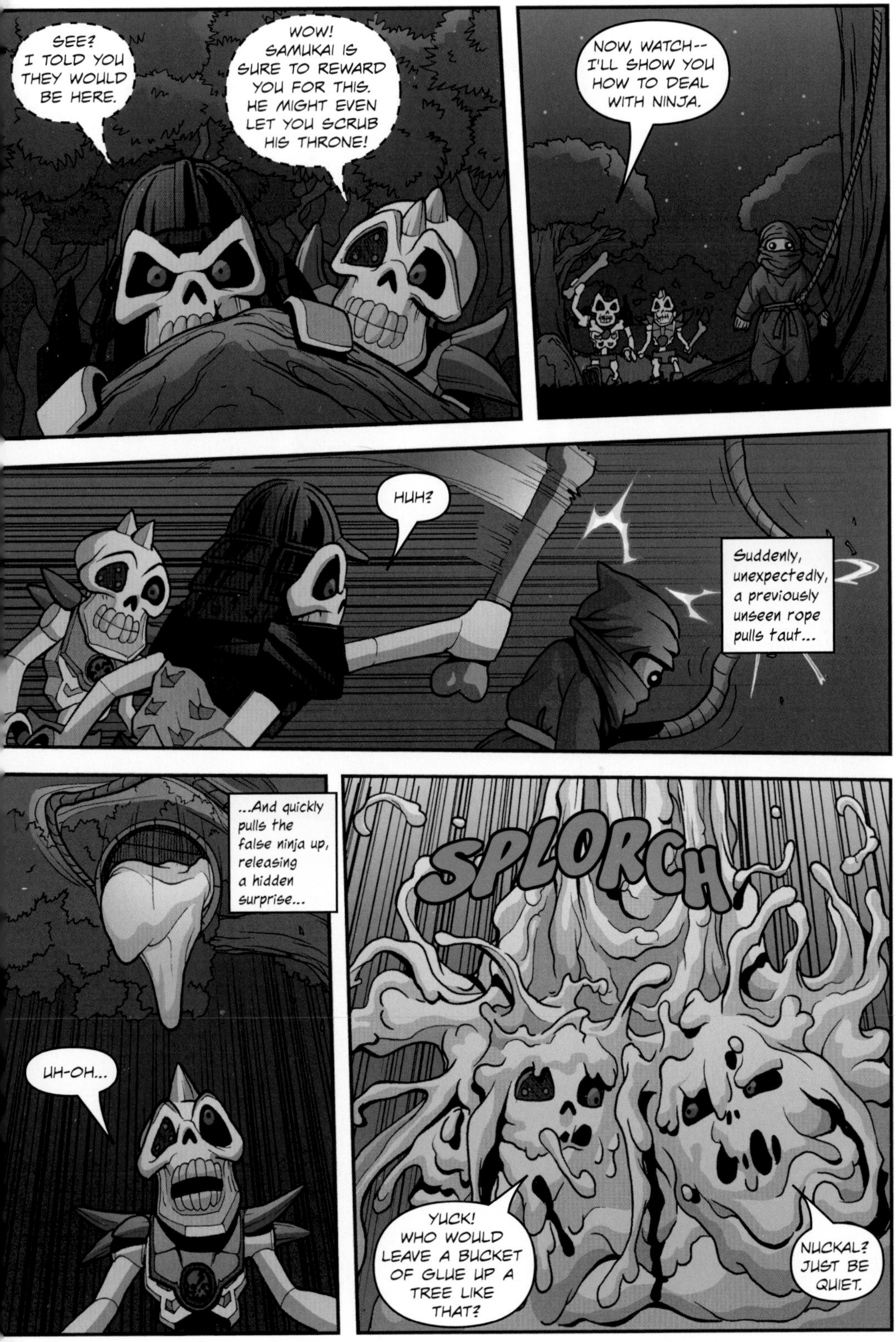
SEE? I TOLD YOU THEY WOULD BE HERE.
WOW! SAMUKAI IS SURE TO REWARD YOU FOR THIS. HE MIGHT EVEN LET YOU SCRUB HIS THRONE!
NOW, WATCH-- I'LL SHOW YOU HOW TO DEAL WITH NINJA.
HUH?
Suddenly, unexpectedly, a previously unseen rope pulls taut...
...And quickly pulls the false ninja up, releasing a hidden surprise...
UH-OH...
SPLORCH
YUCK! WHO WOULD LEAVE A BUCKET OF GLUE UP A TREE LIKE THAT?
NUCKAL? JUST BE QUIET.

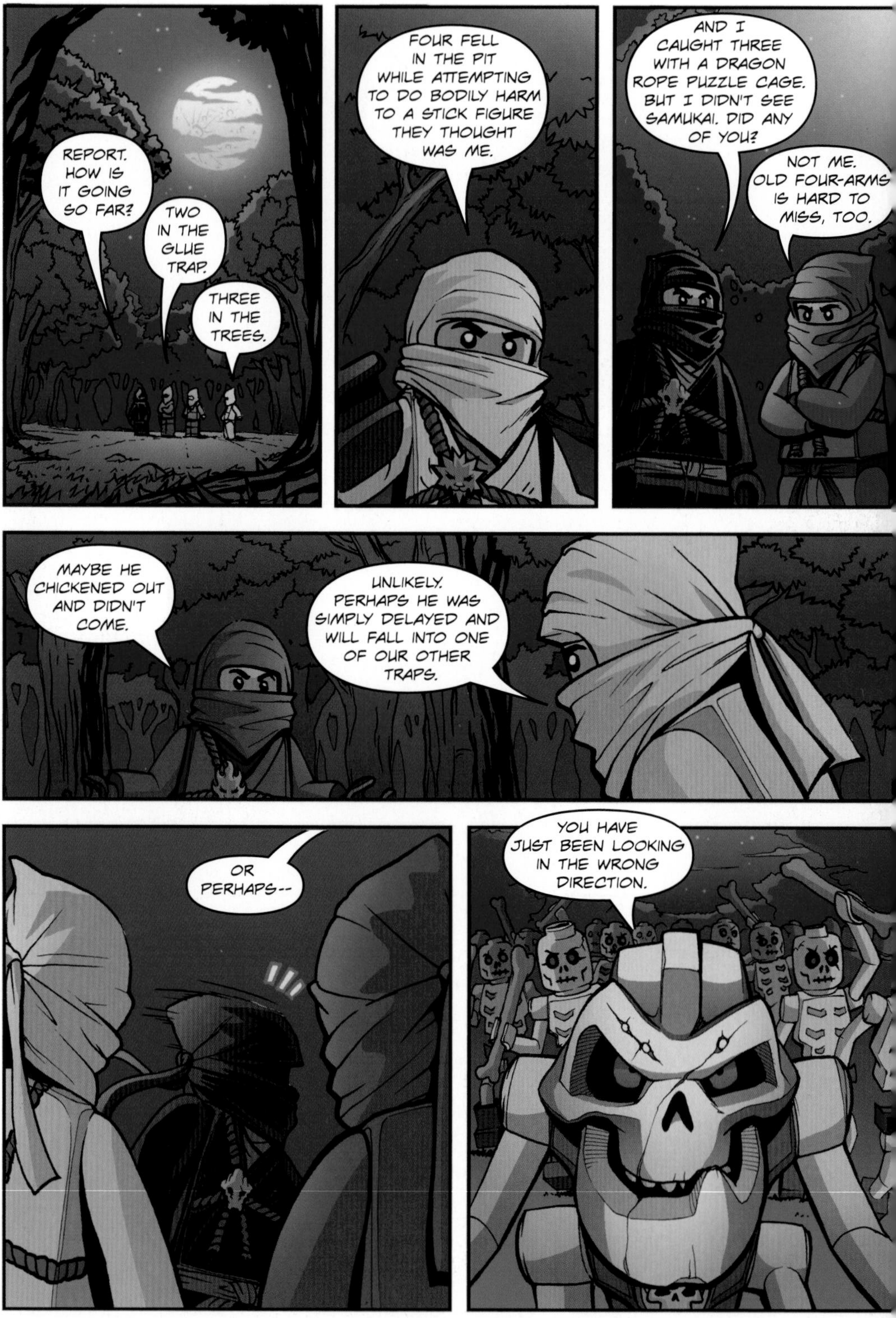
REPORT. HOW IS IT GOING SO FAR?
TWO IN THE GLUE TRAP.
THREE IN THE TREES.
FOUR FELL IN THE PIT WHILE ATTEMPTING TO DO BODILY HARM TO A STICK FIGURE THEY THOUGHT WAS ME.
AND I CAUGHT THREE WITH A DRAGON ROPE PUZZLE CAGE. BUT I DIDN'T SEE SAMUKAI. DID ANY OF YOU?
NOT ME. OLD FOUR-ARMS IS HARD TO MISS, TOO.
MAYBE HE CHICKENED OUT AND DIDN'T COME.
UNLIKELY. PERHAPS HE WAS SIMPLY DELAYED AND WILL FALL INTO ONE OF OUR OTHER TRAPS.
OR PERHAPS--
YOU HAVE JUST BEEN LOOKING IN THE WRONG DIRECTION.

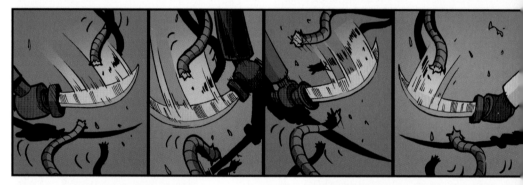

The battle was quick.

Caught by surprise, the skeletons have no time to defend themselves.

Seemingly everywhere at once, four ninja might as well be 400.

Although some of the skeletons also know spinjitzu, they cannot match the skill of Zane and the rest.

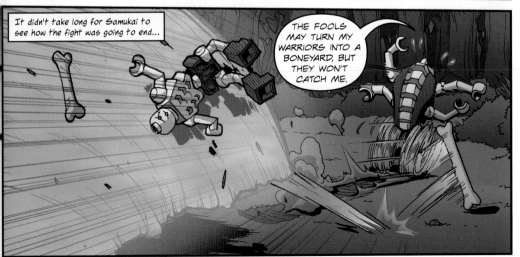

It didn't take long for Samukai to see how the fight was going to end...

THE FOOLS MAY TURN MY WARRIORS INTO A BONEYARD, BUT THEY WON'T CATCH ME.

I CAN RETREAT TO THE UNDER-WORLD--

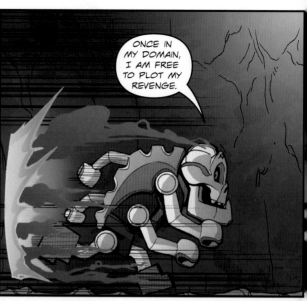

ONCE IN MY DOMAIN, I AM FREE TO PLOT MY REVENGE.

I THINK NOT.

GARMADON! HOW DID YOU--? I MEAN, WHAT IS THE MEANING OF THIS? OUT OF MY WAY!

YOU SET OUT ON A GREAT EXPEDITION TO CAPTURE FOUR NINJA.

AND NOW I SEE YOU, RETURNING ALONE, WITH YOUR LEGION NOWHERE IN SIGHT. WHATEVER COULD THAT MEAN?

A MINOR SETBACK, AT WORST.

WE MADE A WAGER, YOU AND I.

YOU HAVE LOST. NOW THE TIME HAS COME TO PAY.

I HAVE TO GET AWAY. I KNOW THE UNDERWORLD BETTER THAN GARMADON...

I CAN FIND A PLACE HE WILL NEVER THINK TO LOOK.

THEN, WHEN HE LEAST EXPECTS IT, I WILL STRIKE BACK.

WAIT... IS THAT HIM BEHIND ME?

NO. I AM NOT SOME MISERABLE SERVANT TO FLEE BEFORE HIS MASTER'S WRATH.

I AM SAMUKAI! I AM THE RULER OF THE UNDERWORLD! I AM --

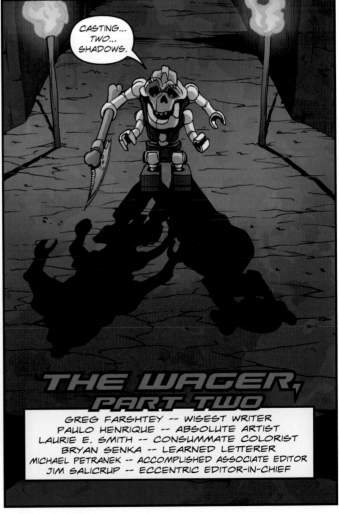

CASTING... TWO... SHADOWS.

THE WAGER, PART TWO

GREG FARSHTEY -- WISEST WRITER
PAULO HENRIQUE -- ABSOLUTE ARTIST
LAURIE E. SMITH -- CONSUMMATE COLORIST
BRYAN SENKA -- LEARNED LETTERER
MICHAEL PETRANEK -- ACCOMPLISHED ASSOCIATE EDITOR
JIM SALICRUP -- ECCENTRIC EDITOR-IN-CHIEF

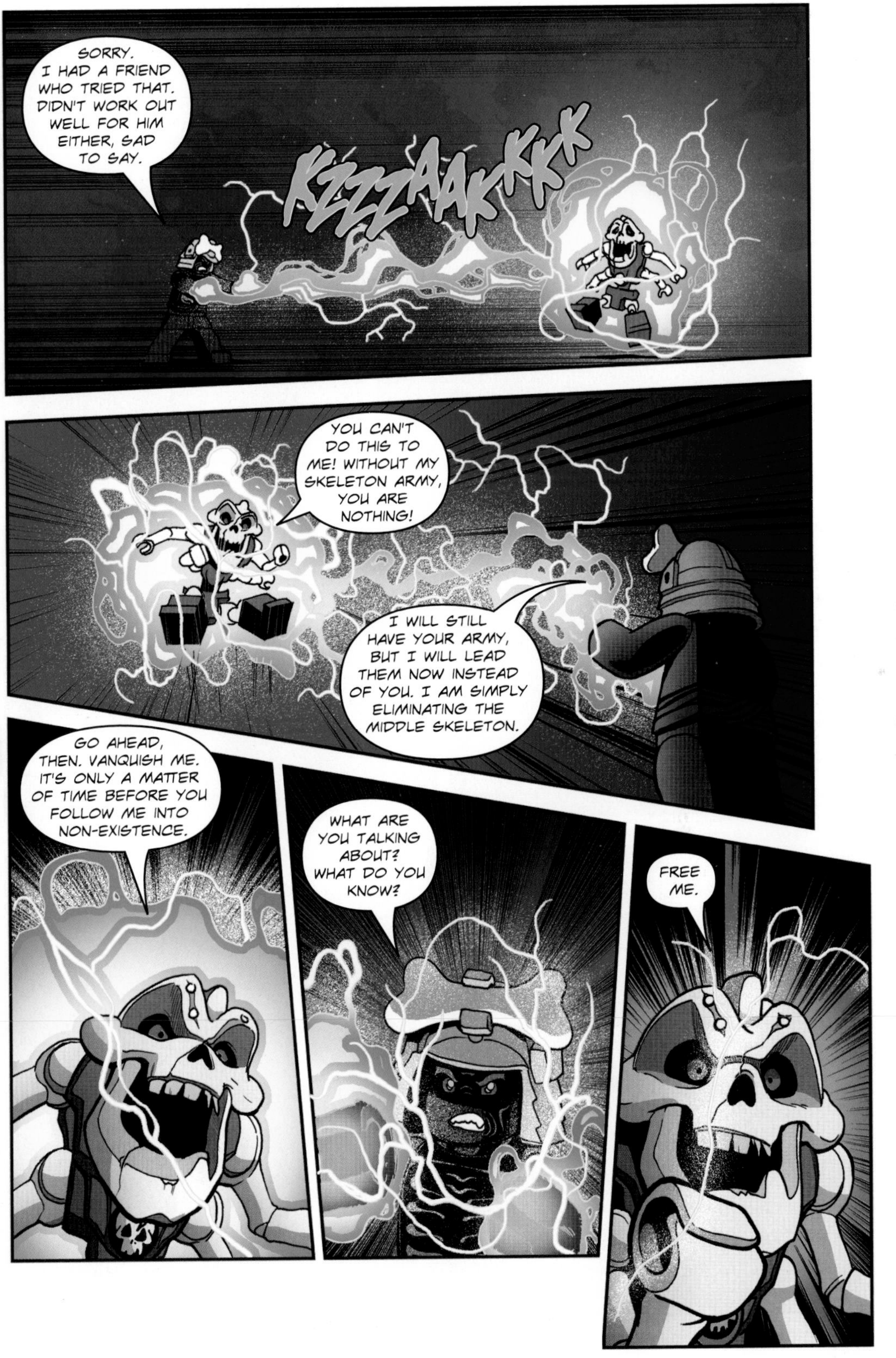
SORRY. I HAD A FRIEND WHO TRIED THAT. DIDN'T WORK OUT WELL FOR HIM EITHER, SAD TO SAY.
KZZZAAKKKK
YOU CAN'T DO THIS TO ME! WITHOUT MY SKELETON ARMY, YOU ARE NOTHING!
I WILL STILL HAVE YOUR ARMY, BUT I WILL LEAD THEM NOW INSTEAD OF YOU. I AM SIMPLY ELIMINATING THE MIDDLE SKELETON.
GO AHEAD, THEN. VANQUISH ME. IT'S ONLY A MATTER OF TIME BEFORE YOU FOLLOW ME INTO NON-EXISTENCE.
WHAT ARE YOU TALKING ABOUT? WHAT DO YOU KNOW?
FREE ME.

VERY WELL.

UNNNGH!

KKRRAASSHH

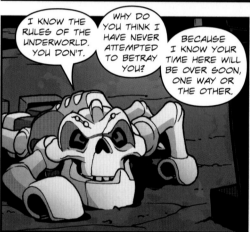

I KNOW THE RULES OF THE UNDERWORLD. YOU DON'T.

WHY DO YOU THINK I HAVE NEVER ATTEMPTED TO BETRAY YOU?

BECAUSE I KNOW YOUR TIME HERE WILL BE OVER SOON, ONE WAY OR THE OTHER.

IN YOUR SHADOW FORM, YOU CAN ONLY EXIST FOR SO LONG.

YOUR OWN WILL HAS KEPT YOU "ALIVE" ALL THESE YEARS, BUT EVEN YOU CAN ONLY RESIST THE NATURE OF THIS PLACE FOR SO LONG.

YOU'RE LYING...

YOU NEED THE GOLDEN WEAPONS, AND THE POWER THEY CONTAIN, SOON -- OR YOU WILL CEASE TO BE EVEN A SHADOW.

I AND MY SKELETON WARRIORS CAN GET THEM FOR YOU. BUT WITHOUT ME, MY ARMY WILL FALL APART AND BE USELESS.

I MADE YOU A WAGER, AND I WON.

NOW YOU SAY I WILL BE GAMBLING MY EXISTENCE IF I TRY TO COLLECT WHAT I AM OWED--

A MOST INTERESTING PROBLEM.

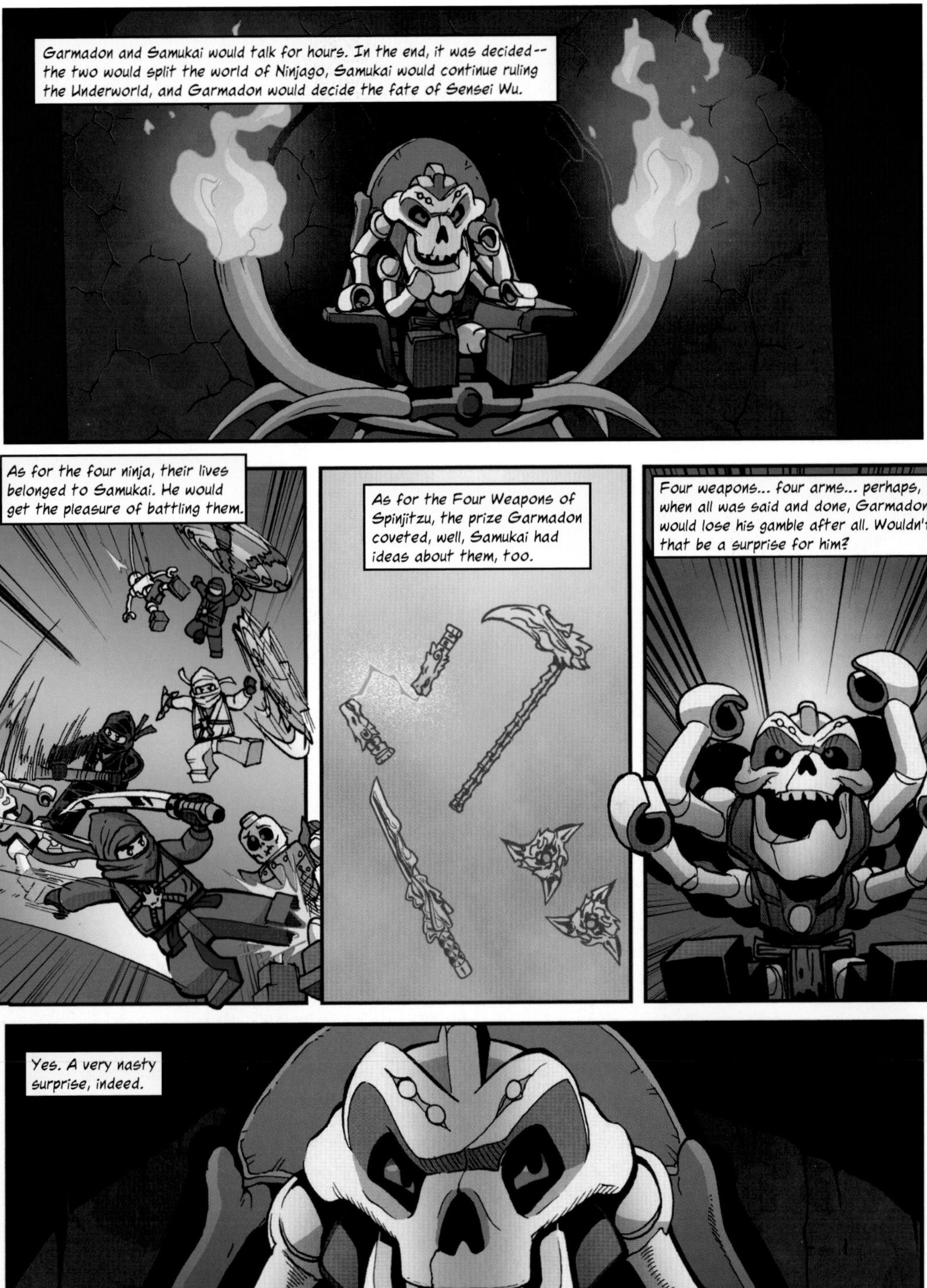
Garmadon and Samukai would talk for hours. In the end, it was decided--the two would split the world of Ninjago, Samukai would continue ruling the Underworld, and Garmadon would decide the fate of Sensei Wu.
As for the four ninja, their lives belonged to Samukai. He would get the pleasure of battling them.
As for the Four Weapons of Spinjitzu, the prize Garmadon coveted, well, Samukai had ideas about them, too.
Four weapons... four arms... perhaps, when all was said and done, Garmadon would lose his gamble after all. Wouldn't that be a surprise for him?
Yes. A very nasty surprise, indeed.

The Four Ninja Will Return in LEGO® NINJAGO #2 "Mask of the Sensei"!

WATCH OUT FOR PAPERCUTZ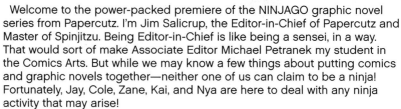

Welcome to the power-packed premiere of the NINJAGO graphic novel series from Papercutz. I'm Jim Salicrup, the Editor-in-Chief of Papercutz and Master of Spinjitzu. Being Editor-in-Chief is like being a sensei, in a way. That would sort of make Associate Editor Michael Petranek my student in the Comics Arts. But while we may know a few things about putting comics and graphic novels together—neither one of us can claim to be a ninja! Fortunately, Jay, Cole, Zane, Kai, and Nya are here to deal with any ninja activity that may arise!

We're also lucky that the great Greg Farshtey is here to write all new NINJAGO adventures for us at Papercutz! Greg built a huge following of loyal fans with his BIONICLE® writing—which included comics and novels—by deftly weaving tales set in the world of Mata-Nui! Greg was able to build an amazing universe of heroes and villains that was so detailed and fascinating, that Papercutz published two separate Guide Books to help fans fully understand it all. And now Greg Farshtey is here to be our guide to the world of Ninjago, beginning with a tale that springs from a bet made by two deadly denizens of the Underworld—Samukai and Garmadon!

Tasked with bringing Greg's script's to graphic life is none other than Paulo Henrique. Paulo had been doing a spectacular job on THE HARDY BOYS graphic novels for several years at Papercutz, and built quite a reputation for drawing in a dynamic fashion that combines the best elements of American super-hero comics with the stylized graphics of Manga. That unique combination made him our top choice to take on the artistic challenges of NINJAGO!

It should be noted, however, that Paulo Henrique, like most comicbook artists, creates his artwork in black and white. First drawing the comics pages in pencil, and then refining his work in black ink, using pen and brush, he then sends us computer scans of his finished work. It's none other than Laurie E. Smith, who actually adds the breath-taking color-- like she did in THE HARDY BOYS. No matter how exciting we may think Paulo's artwork looks in black and white, we're always impressed by how Laurie is able to add a whole 'nother level of dazzling depth and dimension with her creative color choices!

We're proud to have assembled this awesome team of top talents for LEGO® NINJAGO, and we can't wait to hear your reactions to LEGO® NINJAGO #1 "The Challenge of Samukai!" You can either send your comments and criticisms to me by email to salicrup@papercutz.com or by old-fashioned regular mail to NINJAGO, Papercutz, 40 Exchange Place, Ste. 1308, New York, NY 10005

And speaking of NINJAGO, one of the questions we're asked most often regarding the Masters of Spinjitzu is exactly how is "NINJAGO" pronounced? Well, ol' Sensei Salicrup actually has the answer to that one! It's not quite pronounced like it's two words—"ninja" and "go,"—rather it's pronounced as nin-jah-go. But if you've seen the special Ninjago TV movie on Cartoon Network or any of the Ninjago TV commercials you already knew that!

That's all for now. There's more action on the way in NINJAGO #2 "Mask of the Sensei" coming soon!

Class dismissed!

JIM

the SMURFS

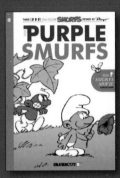

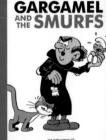

Geronimo Stilton

Graphic Novels Available Now: